TELL ME NO LIES

Samona felt safe in Derrick's arms. Like maybe her world wasn't falling apart. As he pulled her closer, she arched into his embrace. She slipped an arm around his back as he deepened the kiss. His tongue was warm, persistent, thrilling. If this was a dream, she didn't want to wake up.

Slowly his tongue mated with hers, dancing together as though they always had. He should stop. Pull away. Right now. End the kiss. But he didn't want to. Couldn't. Not when it felt so good.

Finally, Samona placed a hand on his chest and gently eased him away, breaking the kiss. Though startled when Derrick had drawn her close, Samona had to admit that she had been hoping he would kiss her. Hoping, despite the fact that she didn't want to get close to another man. Her life was too screwed up for any relationship.

But God help her, if Derrick were to take her in his arms again, she would let him. Let him kiss her. Let him take her to a place where there were no worries.

Derrick spoke then, ending the fantasy. "It's been a long day. I think we should go."

SWEET HONESTY

KAYLA PERRIN

ARABESQUE

★BET BOOKS

BET Publications, LLC
www.msbet.com
www.arabesquebooks.com

ARABESQUE BOOKS are published by

BET Publications, LLC
c/o BET BOOKS
One BET Plaza
1900 W Place NE
Washington, D.C. 20018-1211

First Printing: April, 1999
10 9 8 7 6 5 4 3 2 1

Printed in the United States of America

To my Jamaican "posse",
the Perrins and McKenzies:
Much love to you all!

And to Dane:
Gone too soon,
But always in my heart.

PROLOGUE

It's April Fool's Day, Samona Gray told herself as she glanced nervously around the store. *This must be a joke.* Her brain could think of no other reason why Roger Benson, her boyfriend of only two months, had led her into Milano Jewelers, a quaint jewelry store in Chicago's Near North.

The hand that held hers was damp with sweat, but Samona preferred to blame that on the heat of the beautiful spring day. Anything else—like the fact that he was actually considering engagement-ring shopping—was just too unsettling to think about.

"Roger, what are we doing here?" Samona asked, glancing around the store. Gold, diamonds and other expensive jewelry glistened beneath the ceiling's pod lights. The floor was a sparkling polished oak. Everything was beautiful, and maybe if this had been a time in the not-so-distant past, with a very different man, she would have been excited. Now, it felt like her insides had been churned in a blender.

On more than one occasion Roger had talked about how beautiful a person she was and how much he cared for her, even though she'd told him she wasn't ready for a serious relationship. She didn't know when she would be ready again. Roger had seemed slightly disappointed, but had agreed to an open, casual relationship—no commitments. However, in the last few days he had started talking about the "future." He'd mentioned some investments and how he hoped they'd pay off soon. If they did, he could "settle down" and buy a house. From all he'd said, Samona had sensed he'd wanted her in that future, but this?

"You'll see," Roger said in response to her question. His hand still possessively holding hers, he led her to a display case. This particular one boasted a variety of gold chains. Samona released a cautious breath. Maybe she was wrong. Maybe Roger hadn't lost his mind.

There was only one clerk in the store, an attractive, slightly plump lady who appeared to be in her mid-fifties. She looked like Audrey Hepburn. Presently, she was talking to the only other customer in the store, a middle-aged man.

"Do you like that one?" Roger asked, pointing to a thin gold chain with an emerald heart pendant.

"Uh, that's nice," Samona replied, deliberately not sounding enthused. She wouldn't add that it was too expensive a gift unless he actually offered to buy it for her.

The door chimes sang, and when Samona looked up, the clerk was beside them. Now she and Roger were the only customers in the store.

"Hello," the clerk said. A spark of recognition flashed in her eyes and a smile spread across her face as she looked at Roger. "You've been here before."

Roger's hand tightened around Samona's then, almost as though he was nervous and Samona wondered why. Again, her stomach dropped.

His smile was charming and confident as he faced the clerk. "Yes," he replied. "Mrs. Milano, right?"

She nodded. "That's right. Not only good-looking, but smart too." She looked at Samona as she said the last words.

Samona forced a grin.

"What brings you by today?" Mrs. Milano asked. "Ring shopping for this beautiful young woman?"

Samona stole a glance at Roger, anxiously awaiting his response. *Please let him say no,* she thought. *I can't deal with this. . . .*

"I'm looking for a little somethin' for my lady," he said, not giving Samona the answer she craved. One hand was comfortably nestled in the pocket of his long, leather coat; the other still clung to hers like a lifeline. "When I was here before, Mr. Milano said he was designing some new pieces. Is he here? I'd like to see his new creations."

"Right now, he's out doing some banking," Mrs. Milano said. "Before the banks close. But I think I know what you're talking about. Those new rings are over here." With a nod of her head, she signaled for Roger and Samona to follow her.

Oh no, Samona thought.

"They are quite magnificent, if I do say so myself," Mrs. Milano said as she strolled toward the display in question, her shoulder-length auburn hair swaying gently. "Any particular carat size?"

"Beautiful," Roger almost sang as he peered into the glass display. Releasing Samona's hand, he pointed to a huge pear-shaped diamond. "Can I see that one right there?"

Samona swallowed her shock.

Mrs. Milano smiled. "Excellent choice."

The next part happened fast. As Mrs. Milano began to unlock the display case, Roger grabbed Samona in a headlock. Then instantly, seemingly out of thin air, something cold and hard was rammed against her temple.

A gun. Samona knew it without having to see that that's what the icy cold metal was.

Fear spread through her blood, rendering her ice-cold. And numb. And stiff. If Roger's arm wasn't around her neck she would surely collapse.

This was just so bizarre, so real and unreal at the same time that her mind didn't know how to process what was happening.

Roger had a gun to her head! The image was so jarring it was like she only just realized it. Her chest felt heavy, like something was crushing her, forcing the air from her lungs. She tried hard to suck in oxygen, but couldn't. Her head whirled. Good God, what was happening??

"Give me everything you've got!" Roger screamed. The soft-spoken man Samona had known now sounded loud and hateful.

Mrs. Milano's eyes bulged as she saw the gun, but she didn't scream. Instead, she stood rooted to the spot, seemingly paralyzed with fear.

"Move it!" Roger demanded. "Or I'll kill you both!"

Mrs. Milano whimpered then, a soft cry of protest. Yet her hands flew into the display case, grabbing as much as she could. She dropped the precious jewels onto the counter.

Roger yelled, "Put them in a bag!"

"Y—yes," she stammered. "Th—they're j—just over th—here." Hurrying to the cash register, she cast a quick worried glance at the front door.

"Don't worry about it. Nobody's getting in here, and nobody's getting out. The place has been secured."

Mrs. Milano paled at Roger's words, and it was obvious she was holding back tears. No doubt, she had hoped that someone would walk in and interrupt this robbery, that someone would save her.

Samona had hoped the same thing. But as Roger's arm pressed against her windpipe, as he jerkily moved around taking her with him, she saw her hopes and dreams dying. She saw the faces of her second grade students and wondered how they would react to the news of her death.

Of her murder. . .

"Hurry up!" Roger screamed. "I don't have all day."

"Please. Please don't do this. Th—this is all we have. . . ."

"Shut up and keep filling that bag!"

The pressure against Samona's throat was so great and the effort to fill her lungs so hard, she began to gag. Awful wheezing sounds were coming from her mouth. Each time she tried to inhale, she forced oxygen from her lungs instead. She needed air in her body, needed it desperately.

"Stop that, Samona," Roger whispered in her ear, his voice deadly. "Stop that, or I swear I'll kill you right now."

But she couldn't stop herself. As she gagged, her chest heaved, and as a natural reflex, she grabbed the arm that threatened to snuff out her life.

She felt the sharp, blinding blow then, but only for an instant. Because the next instant, the floor rushed up to meet her.

CHAPTER ONE

"Lawson," Captain Boyle bellowed from across the hall-way. He stood in the doorway of his office like a giant, his large, pale hands planted on his thick waist. His voice easily carried across the room from his office to the office of Derrick Lawson, detective with the Chicago Police Department. "I need to see you in here pronto."

Immediately dropping the file he'd been leafing through on his desk, Derrick rose. The captain had retreated into his office. Quickly, Derrick crossed the open area filled with filing cabinets, desks, computers and bill-boards of wanted suspects to the captain's office. When Captain Boyle made a request—or a demand, as many of the officers at this district liked to call it—you responded as quickly as humanly possible.

"What is it?" Derrick asked as he stepped into the office.

"Close the door and take a seat."

Derrick did as told, sitting opposite the captain's large, cluttered desk. It was always cluttered with various folders, but today there were photos scattered across the older man's desk. Photos of a beautiful black woman Derrick immediately recognized. Samona Gray, the girlfriend of notorious Chicago criminal, Roger Benson.

"She didn't show yesterday," Captain Boyle said, assuming Derrick knew about whom he was talking. "Her own boyfriend's memorial service, and she didn't even make an appearance. Talk about taking the meaning of keeping a low profile to an extreme." He frowned, then continued. "She hasn't messed up once since the robbery, Lawson. Not once." He picked up a candid shot of Samona that had been taken while she was under surveillance, then tossed it back with a snort. Placing his elbows squarely on the desk, he said, "It's time for Plan B."

Naturally, Derrick was sitting in Captain Boyle's office because Plan B involved him. He leaned back in the worn chair. "What exactly do you have in mind?"

"I don't need to tell you that this is a high-profile case. It's not the kind we can easily let die a natural death. Nor should it be. A woman was murdered."

"I agree."

Captain Boyle ran a hand over the bald spot on his head. "The commander and I have been talking, and we finally think we have a way to nail this woman. We've got a special assignment for you."

Derrick was afraid that that was the reason for his being there. "Sir, I don't think I can do a special assignment right now," he began. "As you know, I'm still very involved in that huge heroin bust. I'll have to go to court, and I don't know when I'll be free."

"I'm not asking you." Captain Boyle's stern, abrupt voice made it clear that Derrick had no choice. "As I said, the commander and I have discussed this, the mayor has been involved in this conversation, and we want to find that jewelry. Not to mention solve the murder. We're not going to continue to be made a fool of by some pretty young woman who thinks she can beat the system."

Especially since Captain Boyle's ex-wife, a young, beautiful woman, had made a fool of him by leaving him for an older, wealthier man. Ever since his divorce, the captain had been especially bitter where beautiful women were concerned.

"So what you're really saying," Derrick began, "is that I'm going to do some sort of undercover assignment? Is that it?"

"Yes," Captain Boyle said. Loudly, he cleared his throat, something he tended to do often. "I want you to know that I personally recommended you for this, Lawson. You're the best man I have for the job." When Derrick opened his mouth to speak, the captain continued. "You're a damn fine detective, Lawson. You've proven yourself over and over in this district." He paused. "I know you really enjoy working in Drug Enforcement, but you're the only one I think can handle this job."

Derrick interjected at that point. "I appreciate your faith in me, but I'm sure there are other people in this office, in the city of Chicago, who can do this." It meant a lot that the captain respected him; he didn't easily give compliments. Derrick hoped that would score him some points now. If the captain knew he didn't want to do this assignment, maybe he would assign someone else to the job. "I don't see why it has to be me."

"Are you saying you're refusing to do this?" Captain Boyle's stern eyes met Derrick's head-on.

"No," Derrick said slowly, his hopes fading. "I'm not refusing. But I am hoping you'll reconsider your decision because of my other commitments, mainly the work I need to do on that heroin case."

"I understand your concern," the captain said, his tone abnormally soft. Derrick's eyes must have reflected his shock, for Captain Boyle cleared his throat and continued in his normal boisterous tone. "Look, the mayor approached the commander about this, and the commander approached the captains of all the districts. We chose you. The mayor is counting on you to bring this case to an end, and I've already given him my word that you'll be cooperative. We've taken the steps necessary to cover the work you've been doing in drug enforcement. So that's not a concern. What is our concern is that you're single, you're attractive and you're good at what you do. We need you on this, Lawson. This isn't a question. I've only brought you in here to tell you what your new assignment is."

Derrick didn't know whether to feel proud or angry. He did not appreciate the way Captain Boyle was forcing this on him at the last minute, without even having told him that he might be considered for a special assignment. He was not enthused when he asked, "What exactly is this special assignment?"

"You're going undercover. We need you to get close to Samona Gray." He looked down at her picture and scowled. "We need you to get her to trust you. And when she trusts you, we believe she'll finally break down and tell you where the stash of hidden jewelry is. Only a few pieces were recovered from the explosion that killed her boyfriend, which leads me to believe there's a stash somewhere else. Maybe she'll even admit to her part in the murder. Nothing will bring that poor woman back, but at least we can get justice for her husband."

Derrick nodded. He remembered seeing Angelo Milano, the victim's husband, on the news. He had been so distraught that at the funeral he had thrown himself onto his wife's coffin as it was being lowered into the ground. "How long do you anticipate this assignment will last?"

"We're hoping it won't last more than a month, but we're being realistic. We don't want you to rush the issue. Take as long as you need to get Samona to open up to you. There's no point scaring her off before she's given you the information that we need." Captain Boyle shifted in his chair, something else he tended to do often. "I know you know all of this already, because as I've said, you're an excellent detective. You've done great undercover work in the past, although nothing this. . .personal. But I trust you. In fact, we're all counting on you."

Great, Derrick thought. *No pressure at all.* But he said, "When do I start?"

At that moment, Captain Boyle produced a thick manila folder from the clutter on his desk. How he knew where anything was a wonder to Derrick. "First thing Monday morning."

"Monday? It's Friday evening right now. That's not enough time for me to tie up any loose ends—"

"I know what day it is. Have you heard anything I've said? This is urgent. Forget the loose ends. I'll get in touch with you about your present cases when absolutely necessary. But for now, think Derrick Cunningham. Sci-fi writer."

"Sci-fi?" Derrick didn't even like science fiction.

"Yes. It was the best thing I could think of given the time."

Derrick groaned. Then shrugged. What else could he do?

"We've rented you an apartment in the same building where Ms. Gray lives to make it easier. She lives on the second floor of an old Victorian-styled home. You get the third level." Captain Boyle shifted until he was comfortable. "This is the file on her."

Derrick's eyes bulged at the file's thickness. Reaching for it, he took it from the captain. "All this?"

"Yes. I know, it's thick. I'm sorry you didn't get more notice, but that's the way things go sometimes. Mrs. Milano certainly didn't get any notice before her brains were blown out."

Derrick made a face at the captain's crass words. Opening the file, he said, "This is everything?"

The captain cleared his throat and continued. "Yes. Everything is there from our surveillance of her, as well as

all the information on the crime. You'll need to read that
file on the weekend to get an idea of what Ms. Gray is like,
what she does, where she goes—that sort of thing. Then,
as soon as you can, make contact. I cannot impress upon
you how urgent this case is. And you'll report to me personally on this case, not Lieutenant Grigson."

"What about the Oak Park Police Department?"

"What about them? You think the mayor of Chicago is
going to trust that small, Mickey Mouse force to handle
this case? The suspect may live in Oak Park now, but the
robbery happened in Chicago's north end. This is our
baby."

Derrick was sorry he'd asked. He wondered why the
northern district officers weren't continuing with this case.
Probably because they were too close to it already, and
Samona might recognize one of those officers. It was very
unlikely she would recognize anyone from District Four
where Derrick worked, as it was located in Chicago's south
side.

"Any other questions?"

"No," Derrick replied. But he really wanted to say, "Why
me?" He didn't want to do this. He was knee-deep in a
drug investigation that was more important than this case
as far as he was concerned. Why didn't the captain give
this assignment to someone else? Anyone else?

Frowning, Derrick silently admitted that he knew why.
While he wasn't enthusiastic about this new assignment,
he did accept the fact that he was probably the best choice.
As a single male he was a better candidate to do undercover
work than married or committed men.

Captain Boyle continued to speak, going over various
specifics of the case, but Derrick tuned him out for several
seconds. He flipped through the numerous pictures of
Samona Gray. In most of the pictures she wore braids, but
in a few she had straight hair. Picking up a black-and-white
photo where her hair was straight, Derrick studied it.

She was indeed beautiful. He didn't know where the shot was taken, probably as she walked down a Chicago street unaware that a camera was even on her. Her ebony hair was windblown, and she had a peculiar expression on her face. It wasn't so much peculiar as it was wary, Derrick realized. Almost as though she knew she was being watched, followed, not free to live her life without scrutiny. And in her eyes he saw sadness, or was it guilt?

What had led her to commit the crime of robbery and murder? The answers were not written on her attractive face.

Derrick cocked an eyebrow. Suddenly, he was intrigued. Intrigued about this new case. Intrigued about Samona Gray.

He hated her.

The man who stood above her was large, angry, cold and menacing. His face was red and covered with perspiration. He stared at her intently, his large arms folded over his wide chest, his legs parted and stiff. Every other second, the vein in his neck jumped. That scared her. And the way his dark eyes bored into her made it clear that he would tear her limb from limb if it weren't for the two other men standing in the small, musty room.

He leaned forward, slamming his heavy palms on the table. She flinched. "Stop lying, Samona. We know you did it. Where is it? Where's the money?"

Samona shivered despite the warmth of the muggy room. "I–I don't know. I've already told you . . ."

"A woman is dead because of you. Did you get your thrills when you blew her head to bits? Huh? Did it turn you on?"

"N–no. Y–you're wrong. I–I didn't d–do that."

"Didn't you?" He looked at her like she was nothing more than dirt.

Samona met his eyes. "No. I could never—"

The man cut her off. "Do you want to spend the rest of your life in jail, Samona? Do you? It's not a pretty place. You'd be fresh meat but not for long, not after the women there get a hold of you." His low chuckle was pure evil. "Is that what you want, Samona?" When she merely whimpered, the detective edged his face closer, until his lips were only a mere inch away from hers. "How long does a pretty girl like you think she can last in prison?"

Samona squirmed in her chair, gripping the edges until her fingers hurt. Why was this happening to her? Why wouldn't they believe her? She didn't have the answers they needed. She had told them that over and over, but they told her she was a liar. She was afraid in here, afraid of these big men with their loud voices, with their accusatory stares. Why couldn't they see that she was telling the truth?

"Fine." The man stood to his full, intimidating height. Briefly he faced the two other large men in the room. When they nodded in obvious response to some secret code, he slipped the gun from his holster and immediately brought the cold barrel to Samona's head. "You blew it, lady. Now you're going to die!"

"No! No, please!"

The two big men were holding her arms now. They were going to kill her. She tried to struggle, tried to free her arms . . .

Samona's desperate cries pierced the air. Panting, she awoke and found herself tangled in the sheets. Fighting the sheets off, she bolted upright in the bed. Her body was damp with sweat, and her heart raced as though she'd just run a marathon.

Her eyes focused in the dark room. Recognizing her familiar surroundings, Samona released a long sigh and buried her face in her hands. She'd been dreaming. Thank God. She could relax.

Relax. . . The word brought with it mixed emotions.
While she could relax for the moment, she could never
truly relax. Not while she knew that her worst nightmare
could still become a reality.

She took a few moments to herself, forcing air in and
out of her lungs in an even rhythm, willing herself to calm
down. She could not have another panic attack like she'd
had the day of the murder.

Glancing at the bedside digital clock, she saw that it was
only 3:08 A.M. That didn't surprise her. Ever since the
robbery and murder, she hadn't slept one restful night.
She wondered if she ever would again.

She'd been accused of being involved in that robbery.
The police believed she helped commit the murder.

She was going to go nuts. Throwing off the thick down
comforter, Samona stretched her feet onto the floor. The
polished hardwood floor was cold despite the warm tem-
perature in her room. Sliding her feet into the pair of
slippers she kept by her bed, she rose. Slowly she made
her way to the bedroom door.

Exiting the bedroom, she walked into the living room,
almost mechanically. No longer did she have pep in her
steps. Not since that horrible day at the jewelry store.
Samona did what had become routine every night when
she awoke. She moved to the small window and slowly
eased the lace curtain aside, peering into the dark night.

Nothing. Only the soft rustling movements of the various
mature trees. A few cars were parked on the street, but
not the white van she had become accustomed to seeing
in the last two months. Her racing pulse calmed.

Turning, Samona walked to the plush sofa, the floor
mildly protesting under her weight. She collapsed onto
the soft material and stretched out, staring at the ceiling
in the night-darkened room.

Two weeks, she thought. It had been two weeks since

she'd last seen the van. Two weeks since she had moved into this new apartment in Oak Park, a suburb of Chicago.

Maybe they hadn't found her. Not yet, anyway. But she had no doubt that they would. When the police wanted something accomplished, they pulled out all the stops.

And the Chicago police did want her.

It wasn't that she was hiding. She had nothing to hide, even though they didn't believe that. She had only moved because she wanted some peace for a change. The last two months had been so difficult, so stressful, she needed some time to think or she would lose her sanity.

And she hadn't moved far. Just from River Forest to Oak Park, still in Chicago's Near West. While it hadn't been a conscious effort to confuse the police, she couldn't deny that there was a part of her that hoped they would assume she'd moved far away. Especially the media. It had only been in the last few weeks that they'd slowed down their relentless pursuit of her.

She hadn't even gone to Roger's memorial service yesterday because she hadn't wanted to be the object of the media's scrutiny, and they would no doubt have been there. Unflattering pictures of her would have made the headlines, and that was something she could not deal with. People would have seen her with her new hairstyle and she would be more easily recognized on the street. She couldn't stand that. Not now, when she had found a measure of peace, no matter how fleeting it was. Despite her proclamation of innocence, the people in this town still thought she was guilty.

She *was* guilty, she thought, squeezing her forehead. Guilty of being a fool. She should never have gotten involved with Roger. If she hadn't, she would still have her life. She would have her job, her freedom and everything else that mattered. Now, she had nothing.

A lump formed in her throat at the memories of what she had lost. She would always berate herself for going against her better judgment and dating Roger. He had just seemed so nice when she'd met him at her school. He'd been the uncle of one of her students, picking up the child because her mother could not. Never had she imagined he would turn out to be a jerk.

More than a jerk. He was a lying criminal, and she wasn't sorry that he was dead.

The violence of her thought caused her to shudder. Rising from the sofa, she told herself that she didn't really wish him dead. She wished he hadn't fled town and gotten himself killed. That way, she could at least give him a piece of her mind.

It was still hard to believe that he was actually dead. By chance she had been watching the six o'clock news a few days ago and had learned that Roger had been killed in a boat explosion in Detroit.

Her mind whirling with thoughts, Samona stood and walked slowly to the bedroom, her arms wrapped around her torso in an attempt to ward off the chill that always accompanied the memories. It would do no good to think about Roger, his death and the suspicion that still surrounded her. She couldn't tell him off even if she wanted to, so she had to find a way to purge herself. Somehow, she needed to find a way to get her life back.

Climbing into bed, she pulled the thick comforter around her neck. The bed was big and as she curled into a ball, she felt so small in it.

Alone, that's how she felt. So incredibly alone.

Pulling the comforter tightly around her, Samona willed herself to sleep. But she knew that she would not find any peace anytime soon.

Whack! The racquet hit the squash ball with such force that it struck the wall and blasted back in less than a second. Nick Burns, a fellow Chicago PD detective and one of

Derrick's close friends, extended his arm in an effort to make contact with the ball, but he missed and ended up on his knee.

"Holy, Lawson," he exclaimed, grimacing as he rose. "What are you trying to do? Murder the ball? Murder me?"

Derrick leaned forward and rested his palms on his knees, watching the black ball bounce. "Just playing some competitive squash, man. Can't you keep up?"

"Squash, my foot. Is Boyle's picture painted on that thing, or what?"

Derrick snorted, remembering yesterday's events at the office. As the ball dribbled near him, he reached out and snatched it.

"Guess that means you're pissed."

Derrick tossed the ball in the air and batted it with the racquet. Like a bullet it sped toward the wall then back toward them.

This time, Nick was able to hit it. But Derrick paid no mind as the ball hit the wall and volleyed back. "What I don't like is that I was the last to know. Sheesh, you think Boyle could have at least clued me in?"

"I think it was all last minute," Nick said. "You know the mayor has been breathing down the commander's neck. Partly because Mr. Milano has been breathing down his."

"Mr. Milano is getting on my nerves."

"Hey, he lost his wife. I'd want some answers too."

Derrick nodded, conceding that fact. If he'd been married and his wife was murdered, he'd probably be a royal pain in the department's butt too. "The point is Mr. Milano has to realize we're doing all we can."

"He thinks that Gray woman should be arrested."

"Who doesn't?" The little Derrick had read of the file convinced him of that. "She's in this mess up to her ears but we can't prove it. There was no murder weapon at the scene, so there's no proof she fired the gun that killed

Mrs. Milano.'' Derrick had also learned from the file that the Milanos did not have security cameras installed in their store. A tearful Angelo Milano had told the investigating officers that he was going to do it soon. Now, with his wife brutally murdered, he had decided to close the store. "And Ms. Gray was found unconscious at the scene, with a nasty gash on her head.''

"You think she's innocent?''

"I just said I think she's guilty. But there are other cops who can prove that. Why does it have to be me?''

"Yeah right.'' Nick's breathing had slowed. "Like me? I'm sure my wife would love that.''

Derrick wanted to protest, but he knew nothing to say. Nick had been married for only three years, and had a young daughter. He wasn't going to get any long-term undercover assignments. Besides, he was white—definitely not the man for this particular job. Derrick, on the other hand, was single, attractive, black—and even bore a slight resemblance to Roger.

The fact that he looked a little like Roger could work either way, but the captain was hoping that fact would work in their favor.

Nick patted Derrick on the back. "Don't worry about it. I'll take all the glory on the drug bust when we go to court.''

"Don't even say that, Burns.''

"Then just make sure you put this case to bed real soon.''

"You're right.'' Derrick slapped Nick's shoulder.

"Ow!''

"Man, you're such a wimp nowadays. Must be married life.''

"Oh really?'' Nick retrieved the ball and held it up, ready to serve. "Let's see who's a wimp now.''

* * *

"C'mon, Jen. Pick up."

Samona's nervous hands played with the phone's spiral cord while she listened to the phone ring. Four . . . Five . . .

Jennifer Barry, the only person she considered a friend, wasn't home. With a groan, she returned the phone to its cradle, then sank into the sofa.

She needed to talk to somebody. Jen was the only one she kept in touch with from William Hatch Elementary School. Jen was the only one who believed her without a doubt. Four years earlier when Samona had first started working at the school, she and Jen had become fast friends. They were very close and could talk about anything. Men, the lack of good men and everything else in between. Jen was more of a sister to her then Samona's own had ever been.

In recent months, Jen had started dating. Her friendship with a local accountant was becoming more serious. That's probably where she was this Saturday night. With Ken. Samona was happy for her because Jen hadn't had a decent relationship in years. Still, she wished Jen was available for her now.

Samona closed her eyes, thinking about her friend. She could see her dark, round face right now, her big, brown eyes. If she were sitting here with her, Samona knew she would be cross-legged on the sofa with one eyebrow raised saying, "Girl, you're a lot stronger than you think. Just keep telling yourself you'll get over this and you will. Believe that; hold on to that and have faith. Things will work out."

That's the kind of person Jen was—always optimistic when there didn't seem to be anything worth being cheerful about. Always able to make her friends see the positive in any situation. Always there to ground her. Always there, period.

Jen was the one good thing Samona had in her life. If nothing else, she could hold on to that.

Oddly enough, just thinking of Jen as if she were there with her gave Samona a sudden surge of strength.

Gave her hope that in the fall she'd be back at William Hatch Elementary School with a new second grade class.

CHAPTER TWO

Samona Gray didn't look like a criminal. But having been a cop for seven years, Derrick knew that looks were deceiving. He had arrested many criminals that did not fit any stereotypical description.

Since Captain Boyle had given Derrick the file on Samona Gray two days ago, today was the first day he had truly studied it. "Interesting" was the only way he could describe what he had learned. If there was a type more noncriminal than Samona Gray, he didn't know of one.

Samona was a thirty-year-old teacher—a second grade teacher no less. She was petite, five-foot-four. And she looked like a second-grade teacher—clean-cut, innocent. Hardly rough around the edges, the way the girlfriends of many low-life criminals were.

Derrick stretched his pajama-clad legs beneath his kitchen table and crossed one ankle over the other. Who would've thought that a second-grade teacher would be involved in a jewelry store robbery? A murder? She taught babies, for goodness' sake. Sweet little children who probably thought the world of her. Goodness, couldn't teachers be trusted anymore? Derrick shook his head ruefully. This case just proved that there was no way to really know who was a criminal and who wasn't.

Flipping through the folder, Derrick found and studied the picture of Samona he liked best, the one where she had been caught smiling. What had made her smile? he wondered. Maybe she had been with a friend in this picture, but only Samona had been photographed.

What made her turn to crime? Frustrated, Derrick sighed. Not only was she involved in this jewelry store robbery and murder, but there was a definite possibility that she was involved in two other unsolved jewelry store robberies in Chicago in the past six months. Derrick flicked his finger against the edge of the picture. Two other robberies. . . Was this sweet-looking teacher involved in those as well?

Sweet. Not for the first time, Derrick acknowledged his impressions of Samona. Sweet, gentle-looking. Under normal circumstances, she was the type of woman he might try to get to know better on those rare occasions he gave dating a second thought.

Derrick dropped the picture into the manila folder and rose from the small, round table. He stretched, then yawned. This case had kept him up most of the night.

He may as well get dressed and take his belongings to the car. Luckily, the apartment he would be using for the duration of this assignment was furnished. All he had to do was bring himself, his laptop, the pertinent police files and some other necessities.

An undercover assignment with a beautiful woman. Derrick chortled at the irony of it all. Some men would love such an assignment. Not him. At this point in his life, he hardly thought of women. After his heart had been broken by the one and only woman he had ever loved, Derrick didn't think he'd pursue a relationship for a very long time. As the saying went, his heart wasn't in it.

Derrick walked through his small apartment toward the bedroom, hoping this assignment would not last long. He wanted to get back to drug enforcement, his true love. Not that getting the people responsible for the jewelry store heists and murder wasn't important, but to him, getting drugs off the street was a much more important matter. He saw what drugs did to people, how many lives had been ruined because of them. Working in Chicago's inner city, he especially saw the devastating effect drugs had on that community. It was a community he loved because he had grown up in it. Anybody he could save from the powerful allure of drugs and street life was a small victory won.

After a quick shower and change into a decent suit for church, Derrick retrieved the large duffel bag from his bedroom and brought it to the car. He couldn't help thinking about his new persona. No longer was he Derrick Lawson the detective. He was now Derrick Cunningham the writer. An artist, just like Samona.

As had happened before he started any undercover operation in the past, Derrick's stomach fluttered from a bout of nervousness. The captain was convinced that the best way to get close to Samona was to be similar to her in terms of likes and dislikes. Not only would Derrick be posing as an artist like her, but he'd be posing as a loner with a troubled past. Derrick didn't like deceiving people, but in this case he could justify his actions. One, he was paid to do a job, and he did as was told. Two, lying to Samona in an effort to get her to trust him would help get one more dangerous criminal off the street. Hopefully she would feel a kinship with him. Hopefully soon.

Derrick knew her schedule. Samona Gray, despite the fact that she was a criminal, or perhaps because of it, kept a low profile. She didn't venture far from home, but did go to Grant Park daily to work on her art. Sometimes she went a little farther north along the Lake Michigan shoreline to Oak Street Beach. Samona could be found in either the park or on the beach when working, depending on the number of people in either place.

Grant Park was where Derrick would make his move. Soon he would be there with a notebook in hand, a lonely writer looking for a friend.

"That was a good service today," Derrick's mother said as she spooned white rice onto her plate. "Pastor Rawlins spoke the truth, didn't he? People in a position to help, pattin' others on the back and tellin' them to pray. Why can't they realize that *they* may be the help?"

Derrick, his mother, Sharon Lawson; his sister, Karen Montgomery; and his brother-in-law Russell Montgomery, were gathered around the large mahogany table for dinner at his mother's house, the way they did most Sundays after church. It was the one time in the week they all tried to get together.

"You're so right, Mom," Karen said, chewing a bit of food. "That's what I love about Pastor Rawlins. He speaks the truth, and he speaks it straight." Karen's fourteen-month-old daughter, Emily, sat in a high–chair beside her. Emily was a happy baby who normally loved to eat, but right now she was more interested in playing with the mashed potatoes on her plate.

Glancing at his family members in turn as each spoke, Derrick picked at his food. His mind was occupied. He would miss his family in the upcoming weeks. For the duration of this assignment he would have minimal contact with his family and friends, if any contact at all. The assignment was too risky to jeopardize. He couldn't even risk an overheard phone call from his new apartment.

"Derrick, you seem awfully quiet," his mother said. "You've hardly eaten a thing. Please tell me it's not my cooking." A smile touched her lips. When Derrick didn't reply—merely grinned faintly—she continued, "My baby's not coming down with somethin', are you?"

He spiked a baby carrot with his fork. "Just thinking."

"If you're not sick, then it must be work. Must be a case botherin' you."

Even as a child, Derrick could never keep the fact that something was bothering him from his mother. While he had been close to his father, he had been closer to her. Softly, he replied, "Yeah, it's work."

His mother twisted her lips and gave him one of her sidelong glances, the one that said she was worried about him.

"What is it, D?" his brother-in-law asked.

Derrick faced Russell. "I'm starting a special assignment tomorrow. I'll be working on a pretty high-profile case."

"Really?" Karen asked, her brown eyes growing wide. "Drug related?"

"No. I'm off the Drug Enforcement Unit until this case is solved, and I'm not sure how long that will be. I can't say much more than that, except that I won't be available for awhile. So, if you don't hear from me, if you don't see me, don't worry."

"What do you have to do?" his mother asked solemnly. She dropped her fork and knife on her plate. Suddenly she wasn't interested in her food either.

Derrick gave her a you-know-I-can't-tell-you-that look. When concern clouded his mother's eyes, he added, "All I can say is it's nothing dangerous. But I will be doing undercover work."

"Undercover?" his mother asked. "I don't know if I like the sound of that. I've never heard of any undercover assignment that wasn't dangerous."

"You must be watching too much TV," Derrick said playfully, but his mother didn't laugh.

Derrick then said, "I give you my word."

His mother didn't seem convinced. "I know you hate when I say this, but I just wish you weren't a cop. I worry so much."

"Mom," Derrick said, reaching across the table and taking her hand. "I can take care of myself. I've been a cop for a long time."

"But you can't stop a bullet," she quickly said, then averted her eyes. "I'm sorry, honey. I shouldn't—"

"It's okay. But I do promise you, Mom, I will be fine." Still his mother did not seem reassured, and though it hurt him that his mother didn't accept his job, he understood her fear. It was the same fear that many of his friends and family had, because they knew that being a police officer was a dangerous job. Since the death of his father seven years ago, his mother had become more protective. She was afraid of losing either of her two children.

Derrick knew she was lonely. She never openly admitted that she was, but with no husband and her two children grown and out of the house, she must be. That's why he tried to make it to Sunday dinner with her every week.

Karen must have sensed her mother's fear as well, for she took her mother's free hand in hers and gently squeezed it. "You know Derrick always takes care of himself."

"Hey, at least no one can accuse you of having a boring life," Russell joked.

Derrick chuckled. "Maybe when I'm not knee-deep in paperwork."

Russell shrugged. "At least that's more exciting than quality control."

"Stop complaining," Karen said, her eyes teasing as she looked at her husband. "You can't always have the best of both worlds—money *and* excitement."

"Ain't that the truth," Mrs. Lawson said.

"Mmm hmm," Derrick agreed. Not that he cared about money over his career. He loved his job and was happy as long as he could pay the bills and have a pretty secure existence.

For awhile longer they spoke and laughed as they ate, and Derrick was relieved the topic of conversation didn't venture to his undercover assignment. He was glad that while his family worried about him and the work he did, they respected the privacy that surrounded his cases.

When he was ready to leave, his mother hugged him long and hard, as though she didn't want to let him go. "I'll miss you, son. I hope you're okay."

"I will be," Derrick assured her. He took her hands in his. "And I'll keep in touch as often as I can."

"Please do."

He said good-bye to Karen, Russell and little Emily, then skipped down the front steps to his car.

As he drove away, his mother stood on the front porch waving, a sad look in her eyes.

Samona ripped the sheet of paper from the easel in one smooth movement and crumpled it into a ball. Tossing it onto the floor, it landed atop the other crumpled pieces. She moaned and closed her eyes.

"This isn't working," she said after a long moment, slapping her charcoal-covered hands against her thighs. The black charcoal stained her jeans. Groaning, she heaved herself off the wooden stool and tried to brush her soiled jeans as best she could. She only made it worse.

She scowled at her easel, tempted to throw it, the charcoal and smudge stick out the window.

Who was she trying to fool, she thought, walking to the living-room window. Ever since Roger's memorial service, she hadn't been able to concentrate on anything.

"Ms. Gray, what is your part in this robbery?"

"Ms. Gray, are you faking your injuries?"

Samona squeezed her eyes shut, trying to block out the

memories. She had to forget about the past two months. But how could she, when it was always there? Always there like the scar in her hairline. It wasn't very visible unless one looked closely, but she could still feel it. Thanks to Roger, she'd needed six stitches and therefore would always have a physical reminder of the worst day of her life.

Samona peered through the window at nothing. The street was quiet except for the occasional car driving through. This area of Oak Park was home to many seniors, and she was happy for that. The police would be less likely to look here for her.

More than once Samona had considered fleeing the state and starting over, despite the police orders that she not leave town. If she left town, maybe even the country, she could start again with a clean slate. She had a sizable amount of cash from her parents' estate and generous life insurance policy. Moving somewhere where people didn't know her was definitely an option. If two months had passed and the police still had no concrete proof to arrest her, then surely she was home free. . . .

No, she couldn't do that . . . wouldn't do that. Running away like a coward was not the answer. Besides, if she ran, the cloud of suspicion would always follow her. Any day the bubble could burst on her new existence and she could be dragged into jail. She would be humiliated before her new friends, and maybe by that time even her children. No, running wasn't an option.

She wanted her life back. And that meant staying in Chicago and clearing her name.

Samona turned and walked back to her easel. Maybe she could clear her name by the end of the summer. Maybe she could return to her teaching job in the fall.

Maybe she should stop thinking about all she could not

control right now. Thinking about maybes and what–ifs only made her remember how dismal her life was. Right now, she should go to Grant Park with her sketch pad, the one place she felt at peace. The sunlight, the cool breeze off the lake and other people made her feel a part of something. Made her feel like she wasn't alone.

"He's not dead. I know it."

At Alex's words, Marie abruptly stopped kissing his neck. In the darkened room, she stared at him in disbelief but he stared only at the ceiling. Pouting, she slid her lingerie-clad body off his naked one. She may as well have been kissing a dead dog.

All he ever talked about was Roger. Roger this, Roger that. She was angry too; he had ripped them both off. But there was a time and place for everything. Now was definitely not the time.

"I swear, I'll get that money."

Since the news of Roger's death, Alex was so angry he scared her sometimes. "He's dead, Red."

"He damn well better be. Cause if he ain't, I'll kill him."

"His body was burnt to a crisp, remember?"

"Yeah." Alex didn't sound convinced.

"C'mon, Red. Don't do this."

He dug his fingers into her shoulder and faced her. In the softly illuminated room, Marie thought his eyes looked like the devil's. "Don't do this? Do you think I can let him get away with what he did?"

Marie deliberately took his hand off her shoulder. "If the police are certain that he's dead, why aren't you?"

"Because I know him." Alex lay back on the pillow. "They don't call him The Worm for nothing. That man, I tell you, can worm his way out of anything."

He seemed calmer. Marie placed a hand on Alex's chest,

twirling a few strands of the curly, dark hair. Maybe if she could divert his attention, this night would not be a total waste. When she spoke, her voice was low and sexy. "Why stress yourself over Roger? It's not like we're broke or hard up. We take care of ourselves. We have been for a long time. So if he skipped town, who cares? At least he's the one the police want—not us. This couldn't have worked out better if we'd planned it."

Alex grabbed her hand and stopped it, squeezed it. "He ripped me off. That's the point. I don't care who the police are looking for. I care about the money that he stole from me. Nobody rips off Red and gets away with it."

Marie yanked her hand from Alex's firm grip. This was useless. Exasperated, she rolled over and turned her back to him.

This was not her idea of an exciting night. There hadn't been very many exciting nights lately. All because of Roger. A dead guy who had gotten what he'd deserved.

The whole Roger thing was getting stale. As far as she was concerned they had enough stolen goods to cash in big and be on easy street for the rest of their lives. What was the point worrying about Roger? Sometimes Alex's ego never failed to amaze her.

Alex shuffled then, and the next moment he had his arms wrapped around her thin waist. Gently he stroked his fingers across her belly. In no time Marie was hot. She turned to face him, snuggling her body against his chest.

Alex said, "I want you to find out where she is."

A cold wave swept over Marie and she froze. "Who are you talking about?" But she knew.

"Don't play dumb. His girlfriend—that's who I'm talking about. The way Roger talked about her, I'm sure she knows where he is."

"How am I supposed to find out where she is?" Marie could not hide her anger.

"You're very resourceful," Alex said, running a hand down her arm. "I'm sure you'll find a way."

With that, he rolled over, away from her. Marie knew what that meant.

She had no choice. She had better find out where Samona Gray was, and soon.

CHAPTER THREE

The moment Derrick saw her, he froze. While the pictures he'd seen had enabled him to recognize her, they did her no justice.

It was hard to describe her, but beautiful was not accurate. She was more than beautiful; she was extraordinary, captivating, even in a simple T-shirt and faded jeans. Her straight hair was pulled back and covered with a baseball cap.

Straight, not thin braids like in most of the pictures. Jet-black hair. Shoulder-length hair. Hair that he knew would be very flattering if it was left hanging around her oval-shaped face as opposed to tied back. Like in the picture of her where she was smiling.

Her skin was smooth and looked like caramel. Her eyes were big and bright, and though they looked sad now, he could easily picture warmth there, laughter and happiness. She had full, sensuous lips, lips he found himself wishing he could see with a smile instead of a frown.

Nothing about her seemed evil and conniving. Nothing

about her seemed cold and ruthless. Instead, she seemed innocent and vulnerable, not at all like the accomplice to a major crime.

With her hair straight, she especially looked like a grade-school teacher. A sweet, caring grade-school teacher who loved her students and thought the world revolved around them.

As she shuffled past him in the hallway of the old house, she glanced up at him for only the briefest of moments to acknowledge that she'd seen him. Then she was gone, the delicate floral scent in the air the only lingering proof that she even existed.

So that was Samona Gray, murderess.

Moments later, remembering why he was here, Derrick stepped toward the door marked One and knocked. After a few seconds it swung open and a middle-aged woman with bleached blond hair appeared before him.

"Mrs. Jefferson?" Derrick asked.

"Oh, hello. You must be Derrick." She sounded much more pleasant than she looked. The blue eye shadow she wore matched her eyes, but her makeup could not hide the dark circles beneath them. Her round, pale face seemed wrinkled beyond her years. If the cigarette in her hand was any indication, she was a chain-smoker and that habit had contributed to her harsh features.

Derrick nodded. "Yes."

"Come on in." She held the door open wide so that he could pass, and closed it when he had stepped inside. "So you're the gent who needs this place so badly." Mrs. Jefferson cast him a sidelong glance. "When your agent called, I told him that I don't usually rent the top level. I keep it for family and such, since my daughter usually comes to visit with her husband for an extended period of time and I like to have it available. But then when he told me what you were working on, and that you'd only need the place for a little while, well I figured, what's the harm?" She chuckled. "It didn't hurt that he offered to pay me triple the price. You must be working on some masterpiece."

Derrick smiled tightly as he followed the older woman into the living room of her home. There were cheap ornaments everywhere and hundreds—if not thousands—of magazines and tabloid newspapers. Cluttered did not adequately describe the place. He wondered if she was related to Captain Boyle.

"Sorry about the mess," she apologized. Bending over the sofa, she pushed some magazines to one side. "Please, have a seat."

"That's okay, Mrs. Jefferson," Derrick said politely. "I'd actually like to get the key and get settled in."

"You don't have a lot of stuff, do you?" Before Derrick could reply, Mrs. Jefferson continued. "It is furnished. I told your agent that."

"I've got myself, the clothes on my back and a few other things."

"Hmm." Mrs. Jefferson gave him a slow once-over then, and the gleam in her eye said she liked what she saw. "Very nice." Smirking, she added, "Clothes, that is." She rubbed her palms against her pink sweatpants. "Oh, don't mind me. It's not too often I see a man as cute as you in here. 'Cept when my son-in-law comes over. He's a looker, he is."

"Do you have any other tenants here?" Derrick asked, changing the direction of the conversation. "I'm sure my agent told you how important it is for me to have a certain amount of quiet for my work."

"Oh, just one. She's lovely, she is. Doesn't cause any trouble. She's quiet—maybe too quiet."

"So she doesn't throw wild parties and entertain people all hours of the night?" Derrick smiled, disguising his question as a joke.

"Heavens no. Samantha's as quiet as a ghost. I never

see anyone coming to visit her. Hmm. If you ask me, I think she's running from something, but then who doesn't at some time in their life?"

"True," Derrick said simply. So Samona had given her an alias. It made sense, though Mrs. Jefferson didn't seem like the type who kept up with the current news and he doubted Samona had to worry about being recognized here. "Well, this other person sounds like a model tenant."

"She sure is. She's been here a coupla weeks and if I hadn't seen her a coupla times, I'd a thought the house was empty. 'Cept for me, of course."

"I'm glad to hear that." He had learned probably all he would about Samona from Mrs. Jefferson. "Now, the key . . ."

"Oh, of course. You've got writing to do. Writing a big best-seller, are you?"

"Trying. We'll see."

"Well that New York agent of yours seemed pretty impressed with your work. Science fiction, is it?"

"Yes."

Mrs. Jefferson shrugged. "I don't much care for fiction, myself."

"Really?" Looking around the room, Derrick was genuinely surprised.

"Books, that is," Mrs. Jefferson added as she followed Derrick's gaze. "But I do love my magazines."

"It's a free country. I've always believed that it doesn't matter what you're reading, as long as you're reading."

" 'Course I'll buy your book when it comes out," she said with a big smile.

Derrick shifted his weight from one foot to the other. "I appreciate that. Now, I'd really like to get settled in. . . ."

"Oh that's right. You don't need to hear me rambling. Just give me a minute."

She scurried off into the kitchen, stepping over piles of

junk. Magazines, mostly. A few minutes later, she was back. "Here you go. It's just one key but I do have an extra one, in case you get locked out. I keep all the extra ones here."

"Thanks," Derrick said, accepting the silver key.

"Would you like me to show you the room? It's just up the top of the stairs, when you can't go no higher."

"I'm sure I'll find it." Derrick tossed the key into the air, then caught it.

"Okay. Maybe it's best if you settle in first, then I can show you around."

Derrick agreed, thankful that he was able to finally leave Mrs. Jefferson's apartment. He met with several chatty people on the job and was used to dealing with them, but he certainly hoped Mrs. Jefferson would give him the space he needed.

After all, he wasn't really here to write the next science-fiction best-seller. He was here to investigate Samona Gray.

As Samona shut the car door and started the engine, she wondered about the man she had seen entering her home on Maple Avenue. She'd only caught a quick glimpse of him, but it was enough to arouse her curiousity. He was tall, at least six feet, with an athletic build, and very attractive. There was something about him that reminded her of Roger—the Roger she had liked. Not in a dead-ringer kind of way, but in a more general way—like his almond-colored skin and his square-shaped face.

What had he wanted? He didn't look like the door-to-door salesman type—definitely not the type she had met in the past. Whatever he wanted, he would certainly get an earful from Mrs. Jefferson.

Oh well, Samona mused as she backed her Jeep Cherokee out of the three-lane driveway. She would never know. It was just as well.

*   *   *

When a shadow fell across her sketch pad and lingered there, Samona's head whirled around. What she saw caused her breath to snag in her throat. Certainly she had been thinking about him since their brief encounter, but so much so that her brain had conjured up an image of him?

It was no illusion, Samona realized. He was real. It was the man she had seen at her Oak Park home, his thin lips curled in the cutest smile she had seen in a long time. A smile that was directed at her. She couldn't help the frisson of energy that passed through her.

But she didn't like it. She wasn't here at the beach to meet anybody, especially not another man, even if it was the man from her apartment. That smile, that curious spark in his eyes, could only be construed as suggestive. She didn't need a man in her life—especially not another pretty boy like Roger. Not now. Maybe not ever.

That didn't stop him from speaking to her. "Hello. You're the woman I saw earlier, aren't you? From—"

"Are you following me?" The words came from her mouth before she could stop them.

He smiled, a slow, easy smile. "Hardly. But it's obvious to me that great minds think alike. Who would think that within a couple of hours of our first meeting we'd both be at the same spot on the beach?"

"Yes, who?" Samona mumbled, more to herself than to him.

"Mind if I join you?"

She should say no. It was as easy as that. But for some reason, she felt compelled to say yes.

She compromised. Shrugging, she said, "It's a free country."

The man chuckled, a low throaty sound. As he did, even his eyes seem to smile. He lowered himself beside her on the sand. Extending a hand, he said, "I'm Derrick."

Samona looked at his hand for moment, not wanting to seem too eager to get to know him. For she didn't want to know him. The last thing she needed was a man before she had straightened her mess-of-a-life out.

Derrick pulled his hand back, casually placing it on his knee. His long, lean legs were covered with black jeans, and he wore a long-sleeved denim shirt. She wondered if he wasn't warm in that outfit. As if he read her thoughts, he began undoing the buttons of his shirt. For a moment, Samona stared, speechless, wondering what he was doing. Certainly he wasn't going to strip his shirt. . . .

Beneath the denim shirt was a white T-shirt. Samona was relieved. Men—she'd never understand why they wore so many layers even in warm weather.

He slipped the denim shirt off, draped it across his lap, then looked ahead to the water. His eyes squinted in the glare of the sunlight. Looking back at her, he said, "It's a beautiful day, isn't it?"

Samona managed a tight nod. She quickly realized that he was getting comfortable next to her. She didn't want that. Picking up her charcoal, she looked down at the sheet of paper before her, hoping he would take her subtle hint that she wanted to get back to work.

"You can get to know me now, or you can get to know me later. But you will get to know me."

Her head whipped around. *"Excuse* me?"

Derrick faced her with a charming grin. He looked even more handsome now than when she had first seen him, because his smile touched his eyes. Thinking about it now, she wasn't sure Roger's smile ever touched his eyes.

"I'm your new neighbor," he said. "I'm renting the apartment above yours."

"Oh." She felt like sticking her head in the sand. "Well, I'm sorry for seeming so . . . cold. It's just that I don't usually talk to strangers."

"That's a good rule to live by."

He seemed nice enough, but the last thing she needed was a new, sexy neighbor who wanted to get to know her. She said, "I guess if we'll be neighbors I can't very well call you a stranger."

"Not for long, anyway."

Samona forced a smile, though she didn't like his response. She wanted her space, her peace.

Derrick looked at her and said, "What are you working on?"

"Just a sketch," Samona replied less than enthusiastically.

"An artist? Wow, I'm impressed. Do you do that for a living?"

Samona turned to him then, a questioning look in her eyes. She had hoped that by now he would have gotten the hint and taken off. Why wouldn't he just leave her alone?

He must have read her mind, for he said, "I'm bothering you, aren't I?"

It was then that Samona realized just how rude she was being. Dropping her sketch pad, she hugged her elbows. Just because things had gone badly in her life did not mean she had the right to treat a stranger badly. This man, whoever he was, was only trying to be nice. She at least owed him the decency of replying to him in a friendly manner. She tried to give him a genuine smile, but under the circumstances knew she failed. "I'm Samona."

The moment her name spilled from her lips she realized her mistake. She should have lied. What if he recognized her name? What if he asked her questions about the robbery?

But she was relieved when he merely said, "Samona. Different. I like that."

This time her smile was sincere. He didn't recognize her. He had no idea who she was. Her shoulders sagged with relief.

"So what's a beautiful lady like yourself doing here at the beach in the middle of the day, all alone?"

"I'm not alone. Look how many people are around me." Samona gestured to the various people playing beach volleyball and lazing around on the sand.

"Okay," Derrick began. "Dumb question. But you know what I mean. None of these people seem to be *with* you."

"I came here to work," Samona explained. "You were right. I'm an artist."

"I figured that. We artists can usually spot one another."

"You're . . . an artist?"

"Not a visual one. I'm an artist of the written word."

For the first time, Samona registered that he had a note-book in hand. How she hadn't noticed it before, she didn't know. Now, she was curious about this man who was going to be sharing her home. Shifting so that she faced Derrick head-on, she said, "Oh. You're a writer?"

"That's what I said."

Samona flashed him a wry grin. "Okay, dumb question. I guess what I really wanted to ask is what do you write?"

"Fiction. A bit of this, a bit of that."

Samona raised an eyebrow. "That doesn't tell me much. What kind of fiction?"

Derrick watched a mother happily chase her little boy on the sand, buying some time. He had hoped she wouldn't ask that question. He still found it hard to see himself as a writer—a science-fiction writer especially—and he wanted to sound believable when he answered her question.

He paused too long for she said, "You don't like to talk about your writing?"

Derrick nodded, glad that in his moment of thought, he had perhaps seemed not so extroverted. Perhaps like a man with something to hide. He had to remember that he was supposed to be a loner. Facing her, he said, "You know, I should let you get back to your work. That's why

I came here as well. To write. I shouldn't have interrupted you."

He started to stand, but Samona grabbed his arm. It was a strong arm, corded with taut muscles. "Wait a minute. You can't leave like that. Not now that you have me all curious."

Derrick settled back onto the sand and wrapped his arms around his knees. His eyes followed a couple walking by.

"Hey, I'm an artist like you and I know how hard it is to share your work sometimes. So if you don't want to tell me what you write, fine. It's okay to say so."

"It's not that," Derrick said.

"Then what?" Samona prodded.

"It's just . . ." His voice trailed off.

To say she was curious was an understatement. The man who had seemed quite comfortable with conversation had now clammed up at the mention of his writing. "I'm sorry. I shouldn't pry."

"I write science-fiction novels," Derrick said. He didn't face her.

"That sounds interesting." Certainly nothing too bizarre to talk about. She wondered why he wouldn't look at her.

"I used to write grittier true-to-life novels. About dysfunctional families, that sort of thing. But my agent didn't think it would sell."

Samona nodded. She knew what it was like for an artist trying to do something different and daring in a commercial world. It was a much harder sell than the safe, the tried and true. "And you feel like a sell-out?"

Shaking his head, Derrick finally faced her. "I love science-fiction too. If I didn't, I couldn't write it."

Talk about sending some serious mixed messages. Samona wasn't sure what to think. Only that he was somewhat private about his writing. That she could understand. She felt that way about her artwork. Some of her paintings—especially the ones after the whole criminal mess—

she had never shown anyone. They bared too much of her soul.

Her eyes roamed Derrick's light-brown face. He had the faintest of mustaches and a small black mole on his chin. She didn't know of any black science-fiction writers—not that she knew of many science-fiction writers at all. Finally she said, "If you're a famous writer, then maybe I should hear it from you—not the landlady."

Derrick chuckled, then Samona chuckled too. She was certainly curious and persistent. The important thing was she was warming up to him. "No, I'm still a nobody. I'm not published yet. Trying though."

"That doesn't make you a nobody."

He sifted sand between his fingers. "I know. But I hope to be published one of these days. Soon."

"I'm sure you will be. As long as you're persistent, it will happen."

"You didn't tell me about your artwork," Derrick said.

"There's not much to tell. I don't do it professionally. I t—" She stopped before she gave up too much information on herself. This man was a stranger, and even though he seemed nice, she had best remember that.

"What were you going to say?"

"Nothing important."

Derrick realized two things at that moment. One, Samona wasn't stupid. He sensed that she was the type of person who would only give up intimate details about herself with someone she really trusted. Two, he was definitely wrong about her. She wasn't a snob. At least not in the way she dealt with people. If she felt that her money made her a better person than others, she didn't show it.

"I'm new in town," Derrick said.

"Really? Where are you from?"

"Toronto."

"Toronto?" Her expression said she was surprised. "You grew up there?"

Derrick nodded. "Born and raised."

"Funny, you sound like a Yankee."

Derrick smiled. "I'm good at adapting to different environments."

She rested her face on her palm. "What's a Canadian doing in Chicago, writing science-fiction, no less?"

Derrick faced the water. "Another time." Returning his gaze to her, he said, "Maybe over dinner sometime?" At Samona's wide-eyed response, Derrick added, "Just as a friend. Friendly dinner, maybe a movie . . ." He let his statement hang in the air.

Samona's eyes fell to the sheet of paper before her, and Derrick knew that she was uncomfortable. She wasn't ready to go too far in this new relationship. But at least she had warmed to him. That was a good sign.

There was no need to push her. He had plenty of time to get to know her, to gain her trust. Plenty of time to get the goods that would put her away for a long, long time.

"One . . . more." Derrick grunted as he used his upper-body strength to pull himself for one last chin-up. His muscles burned as he achieved his goal, and he let himself drop to the thickly carpeted floor. He loved working out, pushing himself to the limit, going on to another level. He felt invigorated by this workout, even if it was shortened because of his new assignment.

Because of Samona Gray.

Stretching his arms to soothe his muscles, he thought about her. She wasn't at all what he had expected. After studying the files, he knew she had inherited a fair bit of money. But she didn't look like she had money. Judging by her physical appearance—plain jeans, plain T-shirt, plain shoes, plain hair, plain nails—she didn't seem like the type who cared for a fancy lifestyle. Comfortable was her style, not glamorous. So robbing a jewelry store for a couple of hundred-thousand in jewels, when she already had that kind of cash from her parents' life insurance policy, didn't make sense.

Maybe this look was new, part of her attempt to stay low-key. Maybe she really did fancy the finer things in life. Maybe she had spent all the money she'd inherited and now needed more. So many questions. No answers.

Derrick leaned over and touched his toes, stretching his back. He stayed there a moment, pondering. Something didn't sit right with him about this whole robbery Samona was involved in. Though people who had enough money to live comfortably didn't tend to be involved in unsophisticated jewelry store robberies, Derrick could stretch his imagination and see her doing that. But the murder bothered him. To take such a risk for more money meant she needed it. Needed it why? Was it possible she'd borrowed money from a loan shark, made a few bad investments?

As Derrick made his way to the gym's indoor track, he dismissed those ideas. Samona didn't seem the type to get involved with a loan shark, but one never knew. There had to be another reason. Maybe she'd somehow ended up running with the wrong crowd and had been influenced by them. A thirty-year-old woman being influenced at this stage in her life? Derrick frowned, thinking that didn't make much sense either.

He began to jog, hoping that would erase the questions from his mind. It would do no good to think of her reasons; all that mattered was that she was guilty. No matter how innocent she seemed, she was involved in a capital crime. One woman was dead. Samona had been left at the store alive. If she hadn't been an accessory, wouldn't Roger have killed her too? Why leave a loose end? It was more likely that her injury had been staged, and that she was lying low until she could leave town and freely spend her illegally acquired money.

As Derrick made his way around the track, he gritted

his teeth. There was a time when he trusted his gut feeling, when he knew a premonition was dead-on. But after what happened a year and a half ago, he didn't know if he could totally trust his instincts anymore. As a cop, that wasn't a good thing.

Eighteen months ago, he had broken a rule of policing: he'd let his personal feelings get involved. When Whitney Jordan's life had been threatened, he'd thought with his heart, not his head. He had been in love with her ever since grade school and that had clouded his objectivity. A year and a half ago, someone had been trying to kill her. Derrick had been convinced that her estranged husband, Javar Jordan, was behind the attacks because he hadn't forgiven her for the accident that had killed his young son. Despite the other possible suspects—and there had been a few—he had zeroed in on Javar.

Though he didn't like to admit this to himself, part of him had been hoping that Javar was behind the attacks. Part of him had been hoping that Whitney would realize what a jerk Javar was. Part of him had been hoping that Whitney would finally, after all the years of loving her, return his affections.

It was later proven that Javar's mother had been the one trying to kill Whitney. Javar, who had claimed he'd wanted a reconciliation with his wife, had been sincere. Derrick, who had been hoping to start a relationship with Whitney, had been out of luck. When it came to Javar, as always, he hadn't stood a chance.

Now, Javar and Whitney were happily married and the proud parents of twins—a daughter and a son. Whitney had the family she'd always wanted, and was happier than Derrick had ever seen her. Married life agreed with her. Javar agreed with her.

Derrick stopped jogging and leaned forward, catching his breath. He wanted to forget about the one time in his career when he'd had a serious lapse in judgment. Able to accept that that wasn't just any case because Whitney had been involved, he had tried to put the whole thing behind him.

He had been successful. Until now.

Now, the pressure that had been put on him by the department to solve the Milano case had him questioning his judgment again.

Slowly, Derrick walked to the change room. He made a silent vow that this case would be different from Whitney's case. This time, he would stick to the facts only. He wouldn't let his personal feelings get involved.

Which shouldn't be hard, he figured. Unlike Whitney, he didn't know nor have a bond with Samona. This time, nothing would prevent him from doing his job to the best of his ability, without any biases.

CHAPTER FOUR

More nightmares haunted Samona during the night. She had tossed and turned and screamed and awoken in sweat-drenched sheets, afraid. It wasn't quite six this Tuesday morning, but Samona was too afraid and restless to sleep any longer.

She sat with her legs curled under her on the sofa, a hot mug of tea in her hands. Even after two months of not having to go to school, part of her missed her routine. Getting up at six-thirty, having her morning Earl Grey tea, getting to the school by seven-thirty, welcoming her students by eight. Though teaching had its down sides, there was nothing that could replace the joy she felt when she saw the look of understanding in a child's eyes, when he or she finally "got it." It gave her such a sense of satisfaction, a sense of importance that she could make a difference.

Samona blew on her tea to cool it, then took a cautious sip. It scorched her tongue. Grumbling, she placed the mug on the oak coffee table before her but spilled some liquid onto her hand as she did. God, could she do nothing right?

She closed her eyes, tempted to cry. The tea wasn't the problem. Her life was. How many more days would she feel like this—so utterly empty? Until the official end of the school year next week? Would she then finally forget her morning routine, forget the various lesson plans in her mind, forget her students? Or would it take longer to get over this emptiness because of the cloud of doubt that still lingered over her and her future?

Samona knew the answer to that. She would always feel uneasy until she was free. Free to do what she loved most: teach.

School normally ended this week, the first week of June, but because of two major snow storms in March the children missed several days of school. Therefore, the allotment for "snow days" meant school would end the following week instead. With the end of the school year so close, Samona couldn't help but think of her students.

She sighed. While she missed her job, she wasn't so much concerned about herself as she was about the children. She wondered how they were doing without her. They loved her, and she them. To lose her so far into the school year could be devastating for them. There was so much they didn't understand and naturally wouldn't as far as her situation was concerned. She hoped their parents and her fellow teachers had come up with a thoughtful explanation for her absence.

Samona reached for her tea. This time when she sipped the liquid, it was cool enough to drink. She wondered about little Eric, the one child in her class who needed extra attention. Was he getting the attention that he needed? After a slow start to the school year, he had finally started making great strides after Christmas. At first, he'd been abnormally shy, not saying much more than two words for the day. He didn't have any friends, and the other children could not understand why he was different. Samona had tried all she could but most of all had been patient and encouraging, showing him that she had confidence in him. Her patience had paid off. Eric had finally begun to trust her, talking to her with much more confidence. He had even taken great pride in bringing in and showing her his favorite books from home: mostly about reptiles. When she had read his books to the class, he had been ecstatic. The year-end art unit dealt with reptiles, and Samona had been very much looking forward to seeing Eric blossom even further.

But would he wither without her? Samona took a long sip of the warm tea, trying to calm her nerves. That was what worried her the most. After all the progress Eric had made, with a new teacher she wondered if he would feel his trust had been broken, if he would withdraw into his shell.

She closed her eyes. It was so unfair, the way she had been taken from her class. Not only for her, but for the students. She wasn't like some teachers who only taught for the money. If allowed, she would teach for free. She loved the children, and getting paid to spend time with them all day was like getting paid to breathe. She wanted to inspire her students the way her teachers had inspired her. To touch their lives in a positive way and fuel their dreams. Without dreams they believed were attainable, children could become frustrated and even turn to crime. Maybe that's what had happened to Roger.

Roger. He was also on her mind. Roger Benson, dead at thirty-three.

It was still so hard to believe he was dead, that his memorial service had been on Saturday. After she'd learned of Roger's death, she'd picked up the *Chicago Tribune* yesterday, knowing there would be a story in there somewhere about it—possibly about her. She'd been relieved when she saw the front-page headlines had been occupied with something else: the horrible story of a house fire in the projects that had killed four young children.

She hadn't been able to bring herself to look through the paper for news of the story, mostly because she was afraid she would see a picture of herself. Right now, Mrs. Jefferson didn't know who she was, but if her face was plastered in the papers again it wouldn't be too long before she figured it out. The only papers Samona saw in Mrs. Jefferson's apartment or the recycling box were tabloid papers, so she had felt reasonably safe that the older woman would not discover who she was. But if the media began reporting about her and her suspected involvement in the Milano case, Mrs. Jefferson would surely learn the truth.

All this thinking was driving Samona crazy. She needed to know if there was anything in the paper about her. She couldn't really rest until she did.

Placing her tea on the coffee table, Samona rose and went to the small kitchen table. That's where she had put the newspaper. Even as her hand reached for the paper, she wasn't sure she could bring herself to actually pick it up. Finally, she did.

Carefully flipping through the pages, she found the headline she sought. The heading read: MAN SOUGHT IN JEWELRY STORE MURDER DEAD AT SEA. She blew out a steady breath, then read the article.

DETROIT (AP)—Roger Benson, the Chicago man whose name has been linked to inner-city crime, was killed yesterday when his cabin cruiser exploded and sank while moored at a local marina in Detroit, Michigan. He was 33.

Police had identified Benson as a prime suspect in the robbery of Milano Jewelers and the brutal slaying of Sophia Milano on April 1 of this year in Chicago's Near North. He was also suspected to be involved in two previously unsolved jewelry store heists in the Chicago suburbs of Skokie and Glencoe.

U.S. Coast Guard and Detroit City police have not ruled out sabotage as the cause of the explosion. At this time, however, they concede that the explosion could have been accidental, perhaps caused by the non-venting of gasoline fumes.

A Coast Guard spokesperson noted that boats with inboard motors have to be vented by a fan before starting, to avoid the danger of a spark touching off an explosion.

Samona paused. Swallowed. Nothing had been mentioned about her in the first few paragraphs. Thankfully. She scanned the rest of the article.

According to the Coast Guard, Roger's body had been burned beyond recognition, but amazingly his ID had been salvaged. Some of the stolen jewelry had also been recovered aboard the charred remains of the boat. The ID, jewelry, and the fact that several people placed Roger at the scene, had confirmed his identification.

That was no way to go, Samona thought. Although any feelings she had had for Roger died the moment he stuck a gun to her head, she did feel some sympathy for him. He'd never had a chance to change his life, to try to make amends. And to be burned beyond recognition—nobody should die that way.

She wondered what went wrong. The article had given a few possible reasons, including sabotage. Was sabotage really possible?

Roger was dead. Really and truly dead.

Her name was finally mentioned at the bottom of the article.

Chicago-area resident Samona Gray is still under investigation in relation to the Milano Jewelry theft

and murder. Thus far, however, police have not been
able to positively link her to the offense.

This was a small victory, Samona conceded, a half-smile
playing on her lips. If she wasn't mistaken, the reporter's
lack of interest in her was proof that at least some people
were starting to have doubts about her guilt. She wanted
to jump and squeal with delight, but she stayed seated. It
was too soon for any victory parties yet.

Even though the ringer on her phone had been turned
down, when it rang Samona was rudely startled from her
sleep. Throwing her hand around wildly, she reached for
the phone but it wasn't there.

She bolted awake, realizing she wasn't in her bed; she
was on the sofa. The phone was across the room. It must
have rang at least six times, and it wouldn't stop ringing.
Maybe that was someone from her school . . .

She hurried to the phone and grabbed the receiver.
Before she could say hello, a male voice said, "Samona,
hi."

She was momentarily startled because she didn't recognize the voice. "Y—who is this?"

Click.

She frowned into the receiver. Who on earth . . . ?

That didn't make sense. Who would call for her and
hang up when she answered? She didn't have Caller ID
so she could not see who had called. She dialed "*69,"
but that only told her that the number of the last person
who had called her was unknown.

Dragging her feet across the floor to her bedroom, an
uneasy feeling spread through Samona's body. She couldn't
shake the feeling even as she slipped into bed.

* * *

"Good God, who is it now?" Samona said aloud when the phone awoke her again. She had finally drifted off into a dreamless, comfortable sleep. Groaning, she dragged the second pillow over her head and let the phone ring. When it wouldn't stop, she reached for it, annoyed. If this was the person who had called before. . . "Who is this?"

"Hello, Samona."

Her stomach lurched painfully at the sound of the familiar voice. It was a voice she hadn't expected to hear. A voice she didn't want to hear.

"Samona, are you there?"

Samona found her voice then, although barely. "Yes. Yes, I'm here."

"It's Evelyn."

"I know."

Silence. "It's after eleven o'clock. You're not still in bed, are you?"

"I don't have a job, remember?" Samona quipped.

There was a pause, then, "You certainly are hard to find."

"That's the way I wanted it."

"Even with your family?"

Family. Even now, the word brought a heaviness in her chest and a pain in her heart. She had no family. None that mattered, at least.

"Samona . . . ?"

"How did you find me?"

"What's important is that I did find you."

That was Evelyn—never answering a question she didn't want to. "This is an unlisted number. If the operator gave it out to you—"

"I didn't get it from the operator."

That didn't make Samona feel any better. She'd had

her number unlisted for a reason—to avoid everybody, especially Evelyn and Mark.

"Samona—"

"Evelyn, what do you want?" Just talking to her sister brought all the painful memories of her breakup with Mark surging forth. A breakup her sister had caused. Her sister had never liked her, and the first opportunity she'd had she'd stolen the one man Samona had cared about. She didn't want to talk to Evelyn now. Maybe she never would.

"I heard about Roger. About his death."

"Spying on me?"

"Don't do that, Samona."

"Why not? Isn't it true? That's how you got my number, isn't it? I certainly didn't drop you a note with my change of address."

"I didn't call to upset you."

"Yeah right."

Evelyn sighed. "Why do you have to do that, Samona?"

"Do what?" Samona's stomach was twisted into a painful knot.

"Get so defensive."

Samona stood. "Why do you suddenly feel the urge to be a sister? Out of some sort of guilt?"

"I'm worried about you. Why else do you think that I'm calling?"

"Oh, I don't know," Samona said, sarcasm dripping from her voice. "Maybe to rub in my face what a screwup I am."

"Samona, don't do this."

"Why not? You certainly didn't make any secret of how you felt about my choice of boyfriends. First you said you couldn't stand Mark, then you slept with him. And then Roger—when you'd first called me after what happened, I actually thought you were concerned. Until you made it sound like I was responsible for what happened."

"I've apologized for that, Samona. That came out wrong."

Samona kept going, for if she didn't she might break down and cry. "Even now, I'm not sure you believe me. But then why would you? Just because you're my sister? That's never meant anything to you."

Samona heard her sister groan, and for a moment she wished things were different. Wished her sister had really been her sister in the true sense of the word. But she hadn't been. She'd been her rival, and then her enemy.

"Samona, I just want to know how you're doing. I haven't heard from you in a long time, and I'm worried. I know you find that hard to believe, but it's true."

Samona could not help her outburst of laughter. Her sister cared? That was a joke. Her sister had not cared about her for a very long time. But now, probably because their parents were dead, her older sister felt some obligation to her.

"Evelyn, you don't have to do this. I don't know if you think that this is going to gain you some points somewhere, but I'm okay. Just go on with your life as you usually do. And of course, say hi to Mark." She was surprised her voice didn't crack.

"Samona . . ."

"I'm serious, Evelyn. I'm a big girl, and I can take care of myself. So, don't lose any sleep over me." Before she lost her courage, Samona hung the phone up.

The room spun and Samona sank into the softness of the bed. It didn't make her happy to do this, to shut her sister out of her life. But what else could she do? There was no point pretending that she and Evelyn got along. Maybe for a short time during her life they had actually been true sisters, but that was a long time ago.

Her nerves were frayed and her brain felt like it would explode. Samona immediately punched in the digits to Jennifer's home. It rang a few times before Samona realized that Jennifer was at work. It was only eleven-eighteen in the morning.

Work. Jennifer was probably in the staff room right now with the other primary teachers. Talking, laughing. That's where she should be right now. Should be, but wasn't.

Samona disconnected the line and began dialing another number. A second later, her hand froze above the phone.

A chill swept over her. She had been about to call her parents' home in Dallas. But her parents were dead.

There was no one else to call. She swallowed a sob.

"No," Samona said aloud. She squeezed her forehead hard. She wasn't going to do this. There was no point sitting around thinking about what could have been, what should have been, but what wasn't.

She thought of Derrick, her new neighbor upstairs. He would be the perfect distraction from her troubling thoughts. Maybe she should take him up on his dinner offer.

It was too early for dinner right now. Maybe tonight.

CHAPTER FIVE

Derrick turned when he heard the back door creek open. There stood Samona on the back porch, staring at him as though she hadn't expected to find him here. In fact, she looked startled, as though *he* had intruded on *her*.

After a few moments, she ventured down the few steps and onto the grass, toward the picnic table. Toward him.

Quickly, he shut the notebook before him and placed his elbow on it.

"Hi," she said.

"Are you following me?"

He caught her off guard, and after a moment of wide-eyed shock, her lips curled into a weak grin. "Uh, no. I live here, remember?"

"Ah, that's right." Derrick snapped his fingers.

His attempt at humor didn't impress her. Something was bothering her. She seemed very uncomfortable.

Silence fell between them. Samona fiddled with her fingers, wringing them so hard he was sure it must have hurt.

He was about to say something when she dropped onto the seat next to him.

She said, "Are you writing?"

Derrick nodded. "I'm getting some thoughts down."

"That's good. It's really peaceful here. You can get a lot done."

"Or drive yourself crazy."

Samona flashed him a faint smile. "Yeah. I know that feeling."

"Anything you want to talk about?"

She shook her head. There was silence, then she said, "Beautiful day, isn't it?"

"This conversation is beginning to feel like déjà vu."

She looked at him with a puzzled expression. After a moment she seemed to get the gist of his words. "Oh, you mean yesterday? Yes, you're right." She stood. "Well, I don't want to bother you. I know you want to work. I'm going to . . . pick some flowers."

"Flowers?" Derrick threw his gaze to the flowers lining the backyard fence. They were dazzling in their varying colors and sizes, but Derrick couldn't tell a petunia from a hole in the ground. The only ones Derrick could identify were the pink and white roses. Horticulture was not his forte.

"Mrs. Jefferson doesn't mind. And my apartment needs some life."

She walked off then, to the edge of the vast backyard and the bushes. The white sundress she wore flowed around her ankles, flirting with them. She truly was beautiful.

Derrick made a show of opening his notebook and picking up his pen. But Samona didn't notice. She wasn't looking. She was stooping, sifting through the bushes and picking various wildflowers.

Several minutes later, she stood and walked toward the house. Derrick rested his cheek against his palm and stared down at his notebook. When he heard Samona near him, he looked up, but she merely smiled at him and continued to the back door.

Seconds later, she was gone.

Samona sat staring at the vase of fresh flowers on her coffee table. She liked the selection. The blues and pinks and violets with vibrant green leaves helped add a spark of life to the room.

You need a spark in your own life, a voice told her. She stood and crossed the hardwood floor to the large square window, but the voice followed her. Ever since she'd seen Derrick earlier, she debated going to see him for dinner tonight. One minute she thought she would, the next she figured she wouldn't. Right now, she didn't think seeing him was a good idea.

She wiped her sweaty palms on her sundress. She wondered about him, about what brought him to this particular house in Oak Park. Of all the places he could have gone, he'd ended up here. Jen would laugh and say that this was a sign—a sign for her to get a life. Certainly, he was attractive and he seemed like a nice guy . . .

So what? Roger, too, had seemed like a nice guy. So had Mark.

But Derrick was her new neighbor. He was new in town and didn't know anybody. It wouldn't hurt to get to know him, spend some time together.

Samona had been staring off into space, so mesmerized by the rhythmic swaying of the maple and spruce trees, that she hadn't noticed Derrick outside. She only noticed when he tooted his horn and waved.

Immediately, she moved away from the window. Had he been waving to her? Why had she moved away from the window like a frightened cat? God, he was going to think she was a nutcase.

Well, she had her answer. Forget dinner tonight.

* * *

Derrick couldn't sleep. He lay awake, a hand propped behind his head, staring at the ceiling for a long time. Maybe he should count all the little mounds. Maybe that would finally put him to sleep.

He nixed that idea with a sarcastic chuckle. He'd already tried counting the number of stripes in the orange and white wallpaper, but that hadn't helped him sleep. He'd even tried counting sheep, but that hadn't worked either. Nothing could take his mind off Samona and this case.

She had picked wildflowers to brighten her place. That was just another piece in this confusing puzzle. A woman with high tastes would not get on her knees in the dirt and pick flowers to brighten a room. She would call a florist.

"Don't try to find a reason for what she did." Derrick spoke the words out loud, hoping he could remember to focus on the facts of this case. They were important—not her motives.

This case wasn't going to be easy, he thought, rolling over. Samona was too hard to figure out. On the beach and today in the backyard, he thought he'd made some headway with her. But he was learning that she was fickle and unpredictable. Samona Gray teeter-tottered between hot and cold, friendly and introverted. When he'd waved to her and she'd stepped away from the window, it was like he'd taken two steps forward and three back.

Derrick snuggled against his pillow, willing himself to sleep. Tomorrow was another day. Maybe she would come to him then.

Alex was getting sick of this town.

There was too much heat here with the whole Milano case, and it was time he move on. Maybe somewhere warm, like Jamaica or even Trinidad. With the money he was expecting, he could live like a king there. No more paint peeling from the walls. No more cockroaches. No more bad plumbing.

Marie didn't have to go with him. From the way she talked, he figured she didn't want to leave Chicago. All her friends were here, and her family. So, if she didn't want to leave all that, that was cool with him. It was time he got himself some fresh meat anyway. Marie was getting stale.

She no longer thought the way he did. She couldn't understand him. She complained all the time. Mostly she complained about Roger, telling him he should forget him. But Alex couldn't do that. Roger owed him a huge chunk of money. That money would allow him to leave town and never look back.

Yawning, Alex sat up in Marie's small bed. What was taking her so long? Nobody needed to use the bathroom that long, not even a woman. She was avoiding him. Ever since a couple of nights ago.

Marie's problem was that she was too jealous. She didn't want to find Roger's ex-girlfriend because she thought he had a thing for her. Alex lay back down. Samona wasn't the kind of woman who interested him. She was cute, but Roger said she'd never given him any play.

"Hey, Marie!" Alex finally yelled. "Don't use up all the hot water!"

Minutes later, she appeared at the bedroom door, her face plastered with goop. "What did you say?"

Alex threw the covers off and rose. "Have you found her yet?"

Marie made a face, then said, "I'm working on it."

"Working? Everything is riding on this, Marie. My future. Our future."

"I know."

He approached her slowly. "Then what are you waiting for?"

She moved to the small dresser made of particleboard and acted like she was looking for something, but Alex knew otherwise. She was stalling.

He walked up behind her, slipping his hands around her waist. She flinched. "Marie, I'm counting on you."

"I know."

He cupped her breasts. Hearing her moan, he smiled. He loved teasing her; it was so easy to do. "I want results, Marie."

Leaning against him, she stroked his thigh. "I'll get them."

"You'd better." He released her, left her standing, then returned to bed. Whirling around, she looked at him with surprise. And maybe a bit of anger. He wanted to chuckle, but didn't. Marie didn't like to be rejected.

But he had to make a point: this business with Roger came first. She came second. There was no other way. Once she helped him get what he wanted, he would be all hers.

CHAPTER SIX

Samona parked her Jeep but stayed seated for a moment, waiting until a group of people passed. Looking in the rearview mirror, she adjusted her baseball cap. Never had she worn so many hats in her life, but she couldn't risk being recognized.

Finally, when a man strolled by with a shopping cart full of bags and disappeared, she stepped out onto the asphalt. Instinctively, she dropped her gaze, concentrating on the ground. It was a practice she'd become accustomed to, even when she went to Grant Park to sketch. With straight hair and a hat she looked different than when her picture had been splattered all over the papers and on the news. She blended with the crowd.

This particular grocery store was a small one, half an hour from her home. Although two months had passed since she was a daily news item, people knew her in Chicago's near west. It wasn't only the fear of being recognized that bothered her, but it was dealing with the questions when she was. At the neighborhood corner stores she had been asked so often, "What's happening with the case?" or just plain looked at with doubt and disgust that she couldn't stand it anymore. This drive was out of the way, but worth it for the little extra peace it gave her.

There was a stiff breeze, one strong enough to shift her hat. Before it flew off, she caught it. She kept a hand on her head until she reached the store's doors.

Inside, she searched for the items she needed most. Bread, eggs, cereal, chicken breasts, juice and rice. The store wasn't too crowded and she shopped with relative ease.

She felt like making cookies today. As a teacher, she often liked to bake cookies for her students and surprise them. Shortbread cookies with sprinkled sugar on top, chocolate chip—any sort of treat. Maybe she could bake some for her new neighbor.

Derrick. Why couldn't she get him off her mind? She shouldn't be seeing him, much less baking any cookies for him. Yet she found herself walking toward the baking aisle.

She rolled the cart slowly, searching the shelves. She didn't know what Derrick liked. Sometimes he reminded her of a little boy in a big man's body—his cute smile, those charming dimples, his silliness. Chocolate chip, she decided. He should like that.

She stopped in front of the shelf with a variety of "just add water" cookie mixes. She reached for a chocolate chip package but didn't quite hang on. Slipping from her fingers, it dropped to the floor.

As she bent to retrieve it, so did somebody else. He reached it before she did. The person, an attractive black man who looked fortyish, stood to his full height, smiling as he handed her the package. "Here you go."

Running a nervous hand over her throat, Samona smiled her thanks and accepted the package. She was about to turn back to her shopping cart when she caught the quizzical expression on the man's face. "Thanks," she said, in case he was offended.

His smile immediately faded. Samona's skin prickled and she quickly turned to her cart.

"I know you. . . ." the man said behind her back. It was a statement that sounded like a question.

"I don't think so." Samona fiddled with her baseball cap, still not facing him.

"Yes," he said. He came around to the front of her cart. "I do know you. You're that woman—the one involved in that murder case."

She felt trapped. She couldn't get away. Moving backward, she pulled her cart with her. "No . . ."

The man's voice grew louder as he became confident in his recognition of her. "It *is* you. I can't believe they let people like you walk the streets. After what you did . . ."

His voice got the attention of the few other shoppers in the aisle. Her pulse pounded in her head so hard she could hear it, like a haunting echo. She had to get out of here. Abandoning her shopping cart, she turned and scurried to the door.

"You can run," the man said in a boisterous voice. "But you can't hide. They'll catch you one of these days."

Samona ran until she reached the front door, brushing past people in her rush to get out. A bag fell from a woman's hand as she bumped into her, and startled, the woman yelled, then called Samona an obscene name. Samona ran, afraid to look back.

Outside, the warm air enveloped her and she gulped it in frantically. She clawed at her purse, searching for her keys so she would waste no time getting away.

Away . . . Nowadays, she was always running. She wished she was stronger, strong enough to face her accusers, but she wasn't. She was a coward.

As she ran to her car, afraid to look back, tears of frustra-

tion fell. They clouded her vision as she scrambled inside
her car and drove off.

Much better, Derrick thought as he climbed down from
the old chair, clapping his hands together in satisfaction.
The piece of wallpaper that had gotten his attention last
night was finally back where it should be: glued in place.
After searching the cupboards and closets, he'd found
some glue and had gone to work.

He had too much time on his hands, he acknowledged,
but what else was he to do? Having gone to the beach and
Grant Park in search of Samona and not finding her there,
he had returned home. He'd even left an afternoon blues
concert in the park, and he loved blues. All because he'd
hoped to find her home and make contact with her once
again.

He hadn't. Her Jeep had been gone for hours, and he
wondered where she was.

He cocked an eyebrow. Was she perhaps meeting with
someone regarding the jewelry? Where was it? Only a frac-
tion of the stolen pieces had been recovered after Roger's
death, and Derrick wondered if Samona knew where the
rest was. She had to, unless she'd been ripped off by her
boyfriend.

Maybe she had been ripped off. Maybe that's why she
was still in Chicago, as opposed to somewhere exotic and
tropical.

Derrick strolled to the window and peered through the
lace curtain. From here, he had a view of the wide driveway
at the side of the house. Samona's Jeep was not there.

The flowerpots hanging outside the window caught his
attention. The flowers within were withering from too
much sun. His own plants at home were probably withering
too. Maybe he should go water them.

Derrick shook his head and smiled ruefully. If he was

considering going home to water his plants, that was a sure sign he was bored.

Samona wasn't sure why she was there, but she now sat in her Jeep beneath a tree outside William Hatch Elementary School. She could only stare at the large, old building where she had once been welcome. Now, she was a foreigner here. A criminal.

The incident at the grocery store had only proven to her once again what a mess her life was, how much she had lost. That she would always be running until she was proven innocent. She had driven around for awhile, not wanting to go home, not wanting to go anywhere. She had ended up here.

Remembering ... She couldn't think about anything that had happened in the last two months without getting that nasty lump in her throat and pain in her chest. Her parents' death had devastated her and she'd never thought she could suffer a worse pain. But she had. Because of this case.

Looking out at the large school she loved so much, Samona wiped at a stray tear. Though no children were there now, she could easily picture plenty on the grass, laughing and running happily. In the spring, the primary grade students especially spent a lot of time out on the sprawling lawns working on nature projects or just having fun. She remembered the Easter egg hunt more than a year ago. Her class had gotten so much pleasure out of first painting the boiled eggs, then hiding them for the kindergarten classes. She smiled at the memory.

The happy memory was quickly replaced by a disturbing one. The one person she'd thought would understand her and stand by her was Matthew Hendrix, her principal. Matthew, whom she'd known to be so kind and gentle and fair. But she had been wrong.

She would never forget the way he'd looked at her that day he called her into his office. With suspicion, with doubt. With disapproval.

"Samona," he'd begun, "I'm not going to beat around the bush. With everything that's happened, I think it's best that you take a leave of absence—until everything blows over."

"A leave of—" Disbelief washing over her, she couldn't bring herself to say the words. "You don't really mean that?"

"Yes, Samona. I do. Parents have called the school, expressing their concern. I have an obligation to them."

"But I'm not guilty," Samona protested.

It was only a slight twitch of his lip, but it said so much. So did his gray eyes. He didn't believe her. "Well, until this is all resolved."

"No. Please, Mr. Hendrix. Don't . . ." She hated begging, but he couldn't really ask her to leave the job she loved most in the world.

"We have a teacher to replace you starting tomorrow."

"Tomorrow?" Samona had gasped. Then she had watched, helplessly, as Mr. Hendrix stood and gestured for her to leave. Just like that. Without asking for her side of the story. Slowly Samona had risen and walked out of the room, hoping to maintain the shred of dignity she had left.

Her life was ruined because of Roger. Roger, who had died and left her to deal with the aftermath of his crimes.

She understood now why people turned to alcohol. And right now, she wished she was a drinker. Wished that some hard liquor could wash away her problems. Make her numb. Make her forget.

But she hated alcohol, so she didn't even have that.

She had nothing.

* * *

When Derrick opened the door, he was certain he would find Mrs. Jefferson. To his surprise—his pleasant surprise—he saw Samona standing before him.

"Hi," he said.

"Hi," Samona replied softly.

Her voice was merely a hoarse whisper and he realized instantly that she had been crying. Darn, he thought, not a crying woman. He was no good with them, never had been. Samona may be a criminal, but with her red eyes and soft voice, he couldn't help feeling some sympathy for her.

"Something's wrong," he said.

She nodded, and although she smiled, her eyes misted.

"Come in." Derrick held the door wide and she slowly sauntered inside.

"I'm sorry," Samona said, wrapping her arms around her torso. "I didn't come here to . . . cry. I was hoping . . . maybe we could do that dinner thing you were talking about. You know, that friendly dinner you suggested."

Derrick should have been happy that Samona was here of her own free will. The sooner she trusted him, the sooner he would get the goods on her, the sooner he would get back to the drug enforcement unit. But he wasn't happy, not while she seemed to be in so much pain.

"Sure, I'm still game for dinner. When do you want to do it? Tomorrow? Later in the week?"

"What about now?"

"Now? Oh . . ."

"This is a bad time," Samona said.

"No. No it isn't. I was just about to eat, actually. But if you'd like to go out somewhere—"

"Here is fine. I would actually prefer that."

She glanced around his apartment, and Derrick realized then that he was being a bad host. "Why don't you take a seat." He gestured to the living room.

Samona stepped into the large room cautiously, slowly looking around. Like hers, it was furnished with old antique-styled furniture and beige lace curtains. It seemed perhaps a bit too feminine for a man, but if Derrick was only here to write, she was sure he didn't mind. Like her, he wasn't making this his permanent home.

"I'm still getting organized but take a seat where you can. Just give me a minute." He walked off toward the bedroom.

As Samona strolled into living room, she wiped her eyes once more, hoping to erase all evidence that she had been crying. She hadn't meant to start crying when he had opened the door, but her emotions had overwhelmed her. Now, she wanted to take charge. Take charge of her life and be strong. She'd been so out of control, so emotionally unpredictable in the last two months. That had to change.

She took a seat on the rose-colored armchair. Her new neighbor didn't have many things. There was a pile of magazines and some novels on the wooden coffee table. Leaning forward, Samona took a closer look. They were all women-issue related, and she realized that the books and magazines were probably Mrs. Jefferson's. As she continued to glance around the room, she figured the only thing here that was Derrick's was the laptop computer in the corner of the living room on a small desk. That, and the stack of loose-leafed papers and notebooks surrounding the laptop. His work in progress. His fictional masterpiece.

Like her, he must have come to this place with only the clothes on his back and a few belongings. She remembered him on the beach a couple of days ago, how he had clammed up when she had asked about his writing and how he had seemed somewhat disillusioned when he'd talked about family. Samona wondered for a moment if he was running too.

She heard his voice from the bedroom, but was unable to make out what he actually said. Moments later he joined her in the living room again and said, "I hope you don't mind pizza. I tried to cancel it, but it's apparently already on its way."

"Oh . . . you ordered out."

"Since I'm new to the neighborhood I haven't had a chance to shop. So my fridge is empty. Not much to make a meal with."

"Of course. That makes sense. Yes, I like pizza."

"Maybe later you can tell me where a grocery store is. Since I know where nothing is in this area."

She inhaled a sharp breath. "Uh, yeah. Uh, of course."

Derrick took a seat opposite her on the matching sofa. As he leaned forward resting his elbows on his knees, he smiled at her again, a smile that was totally charming and disarming. For a fleeting moment she imagined those sexy lips on hers, gently teasing, warming, making her feel alive. She hadn't felt alive in two months.

She shuddered, surprised at the thought. That she was having this fantasy about a man she barely knew reminded her once again just how alone she really was.

"Do you like vegetarian pizza?" he asked.

She stood. "I'm sorry. I don't really want to intrude on your dinner."

"You're not intruding. Please stay."

She fiddled with her hands, twisting her fingers, then finally sat. "You're probably wondering who this crazy woman in your apartment is."

"No."

"I'm not usually like this. But right now . . . I don't know. I'm going through a . . . bit of a rough time."

Derrick nodded absently, wondering what she meant by "rough time." Did she mean that it was hard being a criminal? Or did she mean that she regretted her actions? The criminal life didn't seem to suit her, judging by the amount of stress she was going through, which confirmed his earlier thoughts. Somehow she must have been coerced into criminal activity.

"I insist that you join me for dinner. It's never fun to eat pizza alone. But if you're a big eater, I have to warn you that it's a small pizza—only six slices." He had hoped for a smile out of her, but didn't get one. He added softly, "I'm a good listener. If you want to talk."

Samona ran both hands through her hair. "I appreciate that. But I can assure you, you don't want to hear about my life. Now your life," she paused, resting her chin on her palms, "that sounds like something interesting. Something I'd love to hear about."

"I don't know about that."

"You're a writer. That's exciting."

"And you're curious."

Samona nodded.

Derrick clapped his hands together. "Okay. Ask whatever you'd like to know about my writing. I'll answer as honestly as I can."

Samona crossed one leg over the other, leaning back into the chair. "Hmm. . . That's a tough one—not!" Finally, she smiled. "What are you currently working on?"

"That's easy. I am working on the next great science-fiction blockbuster."

"Really?"

"Not quite. But my agent has a lot of faith in me."

"That's great. I'm really proud of you . . . even though I don't know you."

"But you can, if you'd like to."

Samona looked down, picked at a piece of lint on her black shorts, then looked at him again. "What's your book about?"

"Are you a science-fiction fan?" When Samona shook

her head, Derrick was relieved. That would save him a lot of explanation, prevent him from having to lie more than was necessary. "If you don't like science fiction then what I write would probably bore you to tears." He hoped that would satisfy her.

It seemed to because Samona nodded. "You're probably right. But one of these days if you don't mind showing me what you're writing, I'd love to read it. Although maybe you're like me. Maybe you don't like showing anyone your work before it's ready."

Derrick was glad she said that because it gave him an out. "As an artist I guess you would understand. I really don't like to let anyone read my work—except my agent."

"Then tell me this. How does someone like yourself who is unpublished get an agent? I've got a few friends who want to be writers, and they find the process really hard."

"It is very hard and I'm very lucky. A friend of a friend knew somebody who knew an agent and they hooked me up. I was as stunned as anyone when I learned that the agent loved my work. It was only partially completed, so my agent suggested that I take some time to go away and finish the book because she thinks it can really sell well."

"So you might just be the next Stephen King, huh?"

Derrick chuckled. "I don't know about that."

Samona laughed, a soft laugh, a sexy laugh. A laugh that for some reason warmed Derrick's heart. At least she wasn't crying anymore.

She seemed so vulnerable, it was hard to see her in the role of criminal, but that's what she was. Derrick best not forget that.

"I just realized this," Samona said, standing. "You probably don't have any plates to eat on."

"I saw some in the cupboard."

"But did you REALLY *see* them? If you haven't washed them, I can guarantee they're dusty. Do you have anything to wash them with?"

Derrick responded with a crooked grin, and Samona laughed again. That was certainly a laugh he could get used to.

"Then I'll be right back," she said, rising. "I've got some clean plates and some clean cups." She walked across the hardwood floor in the living room to the door. As her hand touched the brass knob she turned and asked, "Do you have anything to drink?"

"No," Derrick admitted, shaking his head. "Well, I have some Gatorade in the fridge, but that's not exactly appropriate with dinner."

"That's okay," Samona said. "I'll bring something up."

By the time Samona returned, the pizza had arrived. She brought two full shopping bags with her. Placing the bags on the kitchen counter, she took out plastic plates, plastic cups, forks, knives and paper towels. From the second bag she withdrew a bottle of ginger ale, a Tupperware container and Ranch and Italian salad dressing.

The plastic plates made Derrick think of an insecure existence, of someone always on the move. Would she be moving again? This time out of town?

"I hope you don't mind ginger ale," Samona said cheerfully as she walked toward the table in his kitchen. "It's all I had."

"It's better than what I had."

Samona busied herself with setting the plates and forks on the table as well as the cups and pop. She opened the pizza box and took a good whiff, closing her eyes as she inhaled the aroma. Derrick couldn't help thinking that she suddenly seemed more alive than she had in any of the pictures he had seen. With something to do, she suddenly seemed happy. Or was it the company?

Derrick didn't want to admit it to himself, but it mattered. It mattered if she liked him or not. He didn't know why it mattered, but it did.

"Well I'm ready to eat if you are."

Derrick joined her at the table and helped himself to three slices of pizza and salad from the Tupperware container. He chose the Italian dressing.

"This is great, Samona. I really appreciate this."

"No problem. I figured you'd like the salad. You seem health conscious."

So she was beautiful *and* perceptive. "It's great. Everything."

"I wish I had something to spice up the salad—some cucumbers or mushrooms or something. But I didn't get to . . . shop . . . today."

He watched her carefully as pain flashed in her eyes. Something must have happened today while she was out. He wondered what.

"Samona, I meant what I said. If you want to talk . . ."

"Let's just say I had a really crappy day and leave it at that."

"Are you sure?"

"Derrick, your pizza is getting cold." She sunk her teeth into a slice.

Derrick followed her example, knowing he couldn't push her.

They ate in silence except for the occasional, "This is really good", "Would you like another drink", "Go on, have the last slice." Little by little, Samona had retreated into her impenetrable shell. Clearly, the happiness had been an act. Either that or forced. She was still polite, still smiling at him every now and then, but it wasn't a true smile. Not while sadness was always there in her eyes.

This case got harder by the minute. He couldn't just arrest Samona and throw her in jail; he had to get to know her, and getting to know her meant he would care for her in some way. How could he not, when she always looked at him like a helpless puppy?

How had he ever let himself get suckered into this under-cover assignment? It wasn't going to be easy at all.

CHAPTER SEVEN

Samona Gray was an enigma, a puzzle Derrick couldn't put together. Long after awaking the next morning, he still lay in bed, staring at the ceiling, wondering. She was so unlike any criminal he had ever known. A criminal he now sympathized with, which was definitely a problem.

"Okay, the facts," he said aloud. He recited the facts of the case, noting the points on each finger. She had the means, the opportunity, but the motive stumped him every time. "Maybe there is no motive because she didn't do it."

Immediately, Derrick threw off the covers and climbed out of bed. Where had that thought come from? Why on earth would he question her guilt? Sure, he didn't know the "why" behind her action, but she *was* guilty—it was up to him to get the proof.

A few tears and he was getting soft. Sheesh.

His instinct was way out of whack. He couldn't trust it anymore.

He slipped on a pair of socks then walked out to the living-room phone and called Nick at the office.

"Detective Burns here," Nick said when the receptionist connected the call.

"Burns, it's Lawson."

"Lawson, just the man I wanted to talk to."

Derrick's brow furrowed. "Why? What's up?"

"I've got some interesting news. A P.I. has been searching for Samona."

"A private investigator? Are you sure?"

"Yep. No one we know of. This guy isn't licensed or bonded. But he's been doing some heavy digging at the PD, calling around for all kinds of information. More importantly, the guy wanted to know where she lives right now."

"Did you talk to him?"

"Nope. I didn't get any of the calls. I just heard about it."

"Hmm." Derrick wondered who wanted to find Samona and why.

"So what did you want?"

"To talk." Derrick ran a hand over his hair. "I've gotta tell you, Samona doesn't seem like a criminal."

"And what exactly does a criminal seem like?" Nick asked.

"I know," Derrick said. "But this is different. From what I've seen, she doesn't have a mean streak, a cunning side . . . I don't know. I just know this is tougher than I thought it would be."

"What—can't see past her beauty?"

"It's not that—"

"Then what is it?"

"All right. There are a couple of things bothering me about this case. One, if this case is tied to the other jewelry store robberies in the last six months, why was there a lot less jewelry taken? The last two heists netted more than four million total; this time the thief only got about two hundred thousand in jewels, according to Mr. Milano. Two, nobody was murdered in the other robberies. Why this one?"

"I hear you," Nick said. "There are definitely some inconsistencies. But that doesn't mean anything. All it means is that this robbery got sloppy. You never know with street thugs. Often, the violence escalates as the crimes increase. That could explain the murder. Or maybe Mrs. Milano resisted. Some people are too stubborn. They're so interested in saving everything they've worked for that they forget about saving their lives. It's sad, but true."

"You're right."

"You know all this. You didn't need me to tell you this. So what's the real reason for the call?"

"I don't know. I guess I was just hoping this would be over by now."

"In four days? Come on—what's this really about?"

"Nothing." Suddenly he felt foolish. Nick was right. Maybe Derrick couldn't see past Samona's beauty and her charm, and was being fooled the way she had fooled many others. "The truth is I'm starting to feel out of the loop. I just wanted to touch base."

"Well, thanks to you, we're all busting our butts on the heroin case to pick up your slack."

Derrick chuckled. "Okay. I won't keep you. I'll be in touch."

"Lawson," Nick said just before Derrick hung up.

"Yeah?"

"There's a rumor floating around that Mr. Milano isn't impressed with how the police are handling the case."

"Meaning . . . ?"

"Who knows? This is America."

"Don't I know it."

"You want to feel sorry for someone, Lawson, you remember Mrs. Milano. You think about what she went through while Samona and her boyfriend spilled her brains.''

Derrick nodded into the receiver. ''Thanks for that beautiful visual image. I needed that just before breakfast.'' But Derrick did need it. He'd been beginning to lose objectivity.

''No problem, man. Any time.''

When Derrick replaced the receiver, he had one thought on his mind. He wanted to resolve this case as soon as possible. He wasn't going to be conned by Samona as Mrs. Milano had been.

Moments later, in an effort to speed this case along, he knocked on Samona's door. She wasn't home.

There was a cool breeze in the air, making the heat of this June day bearable. Samona sat on a wooden park bench opposite a water fountain. Oak Park was a small community, and here, surrounded by trees and the lulling chirping of the birds, she felt a modicum of relief, of peace. Maybe she would come here more often.

Downtown Oak Park was both historic and peaceful. The stately old buildings, the intimate antique shops, the beautiful flower gardens—they were all compelling reasons for her to come here and sketch.

The maple trees rustled in the wind, and Samona watched their fluttering shadows on the ground. Their movements were mesmerizing, and much more interesting than the blank sheet of paper before her.

Maybe she could capture their movements on paper. Maybe, if her mind was on work—not on Derrick Cunningham.

She thought of Derrick's eyes, the way they crinkled when he smiled. They were like windows to his soul, and what she saw was both compelling and sincere.

During their pizza dinner last night, he was nothing but

a gentleman. She knew he wanted her to open up about what was bothering her, but he didn't pressure her. He let her know he was there for her, and that was it.

Samona smiled. Thinking of him, remembering his thoughtfulness last night, made her smile. He was just so . . . nice. She liked nice.

She liked Derrick.

"Mrs. Barry, there's a call for you on line three." Jennifer Barry dropped the other half of her sandwich into the Tupperware container and rose. Walking to the staff room phone, she wondered who was calling her in the middle of the day.

"Hello."

"Hello, is that Jennifer?"

"Yes it is."

"Hi . . . You're a good friend of Samona's, aren't you?"

"Who is this?"

"I'm sorry. This is Samona's sister."

Evelyn, Jennifer thought. Samona's estranged sister. "Hi. Evelyn, right?"

"Uh . . . yes."

"Samona's mentioned you." Not often, but she had.

"Oh, of course."

"Any particular reason you're calling me?"

"Yes." The woman sighed. "I'm worried about Samona. I heard what happened to Roger."

"You did? All the way in Dallas?"

There was the slightest of pauses. "Yes. I'm following the case. I'm sure you can understand that. Look, the point is I'm worried about her, and since I'm in Dallas, I can't very well check on her. And when I called her, she seemed very distressed."

Evelyn had Samona's new phone number? "Well," Jennifer said. "That's understandable. She's going through a lot."

"I know. That's kind of why I'm calling. I was hoping you could go see her today, after school. I'd feel so much better, knowing someone was there for her."

So Evelyn was feeling guilty. Jennifer said, "Actually, I haven't seen her in a while. I'd like to make sure she's okay too."

"Then you'll go? Today?"

"Yes, Evelyn. Right after school."

As Marie hung up, she couldn't help but chuckle. Man, she was good. Alex would be proud of her.

That was a lot easier than she thought it would be. She'd only been guessing that Samona had a sister; if she'd been wrong and Jennifer had gotten suspicious she simply would have hung up.

But she'd been right. And she had not only learned Samona's sister's name, she'd also learned that she lived in Dallas.

Marie threw herself backwards on the bed, kicking up her high-heeled feet as she laughed. Yes, she was good.

Hours later, when Jennifer drove out of the school parking lot and down the tree-lined River Forest street, she had no idea that the black Mazda parked at the curb was waiting for her. She had no idea she would be followed.

Jennifer hurried up the steps to the front door of the house and hit buzzer number two. Since Samona's sister had called her earlier, she had been worried.

Samona answered the door a couple of minutes later. When she saw her, her eyes widened in surprise.

Jennifer grinned. "Hey, Sammi."

"What are you doing here?" Samona asked. She opened the door wide, inviting her friend inside.

Jennifer was about to tell her that Evelyn had called, but thought better of it. Samona might not like to hear that her sister was checking up on her. "I was just thinking about you. Wanted to see if you're okay."

Samona closed the door then wrapped her friend in a tight embrace. "Thanks. I really needed to see you. You're the best, you know that?"

Jennifer pulled away from her and smiled. "So they tell me."

"Well, come upstairs." Holding her friend's hand, Samona led the way.

"The place looks nice," Jennifer said, looking around as she moved to the living-room sofa. Beige was the dominant color in the room, with splashes of rose. Beige wallpaper, beige lace curtains, rose-colored sofa and matching arm-chair and a rose-colored rug on the beige hardwood floor.

"It's okay, but it's not home." Looking around, Samona regretted the fact that she hadn't been able to decorate the place the way she would have liked. She didn't mind the color scheme, but the place didn't have her touch. Didn't, because it wasn't hers. She missed the small two-bedroom house she had rented since landing her teaching job, with a studio for her artwork. But the media had made that place a nightmare, stalking her, never giving her any peace. When she'd finally approached the landlord about breaking the lease immediately, he had happily obliged.

"How are you? Really?" Jennifer asked.

Samona ran a hand through her hair, for a moment expecting to feel her braids. But her braids were gone, gone because she had changed her look. "It's still hard. I just keep waiting for the nightmare to end."

"I called you when I heard about Roger. But you weren't home."

"I unplugged the phone. I didn't want any calls from the media. This was an unlisted number, but those vultures have their ways of tracking you down."

"Hmm. I hear you." Jennifer took a seat on the sofa and patted the spot next to her.

Moving slowly, Samona sat beside her. "I still can't believe it. That Roger is really dead."

"I was totally shocked when I heard the news. I thought about you immediately. . .wondered how you were feeling."

Samona leaned forward, resting her elbows on her knees. "I'm not sure what I felt when I first heard the news. I was so stunned I was literally numb. Then after a while, I got angry. Angry because he had the nerve to get himself killed and leave me here to deal with the aftermath."

"Angry because he can't clear your name."

"Yes. If he ever cared about me, and he said he did, then couldn't he have come forward from somewhere— wherever he was—to tell the police I had nothing to do with the murder? He could have sent a letter, made a phone call. But he did diddly. And you know why? Because this was all part of his sick plan. To make me pay for a crime I didn't commit so he could go to the Caribbean and spend the rest of his life like a king."

Jen's shoulders rose and fell. "Well, he's dead now. He didn't get his wish."

"And as much as I think he deserves it, I really can't wish him dead. With him dead, my life is screwed for God knows how long. Maybe forever. Maybe I'll always be viewed as a murderer, even if the police can't prove I am one."

Jennifer rubbed her arm. "Sammi, you can't think like that."

Samona pulled a leg onto the sofa with her and hugged it to her chest. "How can I not? Suspicion alone caused me to lose my job, to have to leave my home . . . Why I'm even in Chicago anymore I don't understand."

"Because you have integrity. You don't believe in running from a problem. And you want the world to know you're innocent. Running will only make people more suspicious."

Samona looked at her friend and smiled weakly. "You know me so well. Why can't everyone else know me the way you do?"

"Because they're idiots," Jennifer said succinctly. "They're too easily swayed by public opinion."

"Yeah, well, it would be nice if my colleagues supported me. I still can't believe Mr. Hendrix turned against me."

"Politics, my dear. You know it and I know it."

Facing Jennifer, Samona rested her cheek on her knee. Her friend was right. All along, Samona had tried to blame Mr. Hendrix for his actions, but he wasn't free to make the choices he made. Not without the scrutiny of the board and parents. Given the circumstances, he'd really had no other choice to make. Still, privately he could have told her he was behind her. The fact that he hadn't meant that he wasn't.

"Don't do it," Jennifer warned. "Don't . . ."

But Samona couldn't help it. The hopelessness of the situation hit her, and tears fell from her eyes. Lifting her head, she brushed them away.

"Listen to me, Sammi. Life is full of challenges, of ups and downs. You accept and appreciate the good times, but you can't run from the bad. You deal with them and go on."

"How can I go on when this cloud of doom is hanging over my head?"

Jennifer gently squeezed Samona's shoulder. "You can't think like that. You have to think that no matter how dark and frightening the night is, the sun always rises in the morning."

Samona grinned through her tears. "What would I do without you?"

"Oh . . ." Jennifer paused, searching for words. She finally flashed a weak smile and said, "You'd be fine. I'm sure of it."

Samona nodded, feeling stronger now. Jennifer was right. Somehow, this horrible night would finally end.

"Now," Jennifer began, pushing herself off the sofa. "Sit tight. I'll make us dinner."

"Okay." Samona ran the back of her hand across her face, making herself presentable.

Several seconds later, Jennifer called from the kitchen, "I guess we have to order in. You've got nothing but milk and margarine in here."

"Oh, that's right," Samona called back. "I forgot to do some shopping."

Jennifer was at the living-room entrance then, her hands on her hips in a motherly scold. The next second, she giggled. "How does Chinese sound?"

"Perfect."

Hours later, Samona and Jennifer stood in the house's doorway, saying their good-byes.

Jennifer reached for the door, but it opened before she could turn the knob. Gasping a little, she stepped backwards before the door hit her.

"Oh, hi," she said when Derrick stepped into the foyer, raising a curious eyebrow.

"Hi," Derrick replied, smiling politely. "Samona."

Samona grinned. Derrick didn't stop to chat, but rather made his way to the steps and then up the stairs.

"Whew!" Jennifer said when he was out of earshot, fanning herself with her hand. "Who was that?"

"Derrick. My new neighbor. He's renting the top floor."

Jennifer's eyes lit up. "Then what I said about your days getting brighter, I think that's going to happen a lot sooner than I thought." She giggled.

"Get out of here," Samona said, giggling too.

"Good night."

There was a faint knock on the door, and when Samona heard it, her heart rate sped up. It was either Derrick or Mrs. Jefferson. She hoped it was Derrick.

It was. "Hi," Samona said softly.

"Hey, Samona. Is your friend still here?"

Samona shook her head. If Mark had asked her that question, she would have wondered if he were interested in Jennifer. With Derrick, it was different. She knew he was asking only because he was curious. "No. She left about an hour ago."

"In that case, I was wondering if you had any plans for the evening. And if not, maybe you'd like to spend some time with me. I was thinking of maybe a walk on the beach or maybe even a movie. I think the blues festival is going on in Grant Park. . . ."

He really did have nice eyes. Striking, hazel eyes. Just the way he looked at her made her skin warm. Samona wondered if maybe she was coming down with something.

"Samona?"

"Tonight isn't a good night," she finally replied. Derrick was dangerous. She should stay away from him.

"Oh." Derrick tried to mask his disappointment, but she saw it in his eyes. "Okay. I'll see you later."

He turned and started to walk away when Samona said, "Wait."

Derrick spun around. "Yes?"

God, she was crazy. Crazy for even considering spending more time with Derrick. But she liked him. She couldn't deny that.

"Tonight isn't really a great night, but I was thinking about tomorrow. Maybe we could check out Ernest Hemingway's birthplace. You know, since you're a writer and he was a writer. After all, you are in Oak Park—the place where he grew up."

"Tomorrow?"

"If you're busy . . ."

"I'm not."

"So, what do you say?" Samona hoped he would say yes.

"I can't wait."

A smile touched her lips. Doing something with Derrick—anything—was better than sitting at home feeling sorry for herself.

"I found her."

Alex's face lit up with a genuine smile and he pulled Marie into his arms. "Come here."

He kissed her long and hard, his hands traveling over her body. "I knew you could do it."

Marie shrugged out of his embrace and walked toward the living-room window. Alex had been so up and down lately, one minute hot, the next cold, Marie didn't know what to think. Maybe she was overreacting, but she felt like she was being used.

"What's your problem?" Alex's voice was no longer sweet, but harsh.

"Why do you want to find her so badly, anyway? You have a thing for her?"

"Don't play jealous. It doesn't suit you."

"What am I supposed to think?"

Alex moved toward her then, and once again took her in his arms. "You're supposed to think that I'm looking out for you. That's why all this is so important to me. Samona means nothing to me. It's the jewelry I care about."

Marie pouted then looked into his dark eyes. Lifting a hand to his face, she stroked his dark skin. She really did love her man and didn't want to share him with anybody. "You sure?"

"Of course I'm sure. This jewelry is our ticket to a very secure future. Once we get the money we deserve, all our dreams will come true."

Surrendering to his kiss, Marie prayed that was true.

CHAPTER EIGHT

Ernest Hemingway's birthplace was a beautiful Victorian Queen Anne–styled home on Oak Park Avenue in Oak Park. The house had been refurbished to look as close to the original as possible, a project that was ongoing. Everything looked fabulous, from the fireplace with a carved oak mantle in the parlor to the rose-patterned cornice moldings on the main level.

Samona loved old houses. In this one, the mix and match of designs in the living room—the green-and-white striped wallpaper with a floral border, the Nottingham lace curtains, the flowered carpeting—strangely matched. Definitely, the odd combination added character. Old houses had so much more mystery than modern ones.

Samona especially liked Grace Hemingway's bedroom, which was one of the rooms that had been completely renovated. It looked just as it had in the late 1800s—there was even an original picture of the room as it had been then, to which visitors could compare the new version. Everything was accurate. The room was very feminine, with a dressing table draped in white organdy and a beautiful iron bed. Lace even hung over the dressing table mirror, pulled back like curtains. Adjoining the room was the nursery where Hemingway had spent his first few years.

Derrick seemed genuinely intrigued. He, Samona and a few tourists spent a good part of the afternoon touring the various rooms of the house and watching videos about the Hemingway family life. It had been like taking a step back in time.

The director of the house was a pleasant older woman who was sincere in her excitement for the house and Hemingway's work. She extended an invitation for them to return whenever they desired. As Derrick and Samona left, she stood on the porch waving.

Samona slipped into the passenger's seat in Derrick's white Honda, glad that he had parked under a sprawling maple tree that provided ample shade. She rolled down her window. "To think I've lived here how long and have never checked out Hemingway's birthplace."

"I don't know what it was like before, but the renovated version looked great. Really authentic. Though I don't think I could have lived back then."

"Why not?" Samona challenged.

Derrick raised an eyebrow. "I kinda like modern plumbing."

"Oh. Me too."

Derrick slipped the key into the ignition. "How about some lunch?"

"Sure."

"What do you feel like?"

Samona pursed her lips. "Hmm. Anything. I'm easy."

Derrick turned to her and said, "I hope not."

Her face grew hot. But strangely, Derrick's comment stirred a desire within her she'd long thought dead. "I didn't mean it that way."

"I know. Bad joke." Derrick started the car and the

engine of his late-model Honda purred. "Since I haven't seen much of downtown Oak Park, I wouldn't mind checking it out now." That was true. He didn't live in this part of Chicago and didn't get here much.

"There are a lot of neat little shops down there, and a few great places to eat."

"Sounds good. Let's go."

Within minutes, they were parked and out of the car in downtown Oak Park. Samona swallowed hard. Though she'd found nothing but peace here before, she suddenly worried about being recognized. She couldn't handle a repeat of the grocery-store incident with Derrick around.

"Are you okay?" Derrick asked.

His voice brought her out of her thoughts. No, she wasn't okay. But how could she tell him that she just wanted to go home now? She couldn't. Inhaling a deep breath of the warm summer air, Samona stepped away from the car. "I'm fine. I was just . . . lost in my thoughts for a moment."

"You sure?"

"Mmm hmm."

She was trying to be strong, Derrick knew. For a moment he felt guilty about doing this to her. Obviously, she was uncomfortable in public. At Hemingway's house, she hadn't taken off her floppy hat; she'd even angled it over her forehead to obscure her face. She didn't want to be recognized. Who would, if they had done what she had done?

They found a small, quaint deli with a patio and an awning that provided shade. They both ordered turkey on a Kaiser roll and juice. At their table, Samona took a seat with her back facing the street.

"So," she said, lifting her sandwich. "How does Chicago compare to Toronto?"

Derrick washed down his food with his orange juice. "Chicago's cool. I like it."

"Yeah, me too."

"Have you ever been to Toronto?"

Samona shook her head. "Never. But I've heard lots of great things about it."

"It's a great place." That much Derrick could say with confidence. He had been to Toronto before with his family, even if it was several years ago.

"When do you plan on returning?"

Derrick didn't answer right away. Partly because he had bitten off a piece of his sandwich. Partly because he wanted to make Samona wonder. "I don't know."

"You must know how long you plan on renting the place in Chicago . . ."

"As long as is necessary."

Just like before, Derrick had shut down when Samona asked about himself. More and more she knew he had something to hide. What was he running from? Something as horrible as she was?

She wanted to find out. Wanted to, because maybe she and Derrick had more in common than he knew. If she could get him to trust her with his story, maybe she could trust him with hers. Maybe she could ease her burden.

"Remember what you told me the other night? About you being willing to listen to me if I had anything to say? The same goes for me. I'm a good listener as well."

"There's nothing to say."

He couldn't even look at her as he said the words. But Samona understood. Some things just weren't easy to talk about. As he had with her, she gave him his space.

"I guess I'm not the only one who's had a rough time."

"No, you're not."

Samona didn't know what else to say. She couldn't very well expect him to open up when she hadn't. As a result, they both ate in comfortable silence. Although they were more like strangers because they didn't really know much about each other, it seemed to Samona that they were becoming friends.

* * *

When Derrick returned home, his answering machine was flashing. It had to be work. Nobody else had his phone number here. Hitting the play button, the machine whirred softly as it rewound.

"Boyles here." The captain's loud voice filled the small bedroom. "We need to talk ASAP. We may have a big problem with this case. Milano's lawyer contacted the commander today. He gave the department a stupid ultimatum, saying that if we don't solve this case in a week, he's going to sue us. The commander isn't happy, and neither am I. The heat is on, Lawson, and I can only hope you're making progress. Call me and let me know what's happening."

The message ended with a series of loud beeps. Derrick groaned. The captain's message was the last thing he needed to hear. He had tried his best, but was no closer to solving this case than when he had started.

Already anticipating Captain Boyle's reaction to his news, Derrick reluctantly picked up the phone and dialed.

It seemed the nightmare was just beginning.

Long after Samona had returned home, she sat huddled on one corner of her sofa, trembling. She was so cold, no heat could warm her. She was so confused, she didn't know what to do. And she was so afraid.

The cause of her fear lay at the bottom of the garbage can in her kitchen, ripped into several tiny pieces.

One minute she had been happy, the next terrified. That was how quickly things could change, she knew. In an instant.

It had taken only an instant for her to return home and see the note slipped under her door. It had been written on a letter-size piece of paper, folded twice. At first, she'd thought it was a note from Mrs. Jefferson. As she read it, she'd learned otherwise.

For a moment, she had only been able to stand and stare. Stare as her body quivered. The unsigned note told her in big, bold letters that she had been found. She was being watched. The person who wrote the note wanted the jewelry Roger had stolen.

Samona closed her eyes, placed her chin on her knees. If this was all a bad dream, why wouldn't it end? She knew nothing about the jewelry, knew nothing about the murder. Why did nobody—except Jennifer—believe her?

Until now, it hadn't occurred to her that Roger had been working with somebody else, but it made sense. He couldn't have pulled off such a crime alone. That's what the police believed; it was why they suspected her. Now, Samona knew Roger had worked with a partner. Maybe more than one.

She should have known. Maybe she had heard something, seen something, but she'd drawn a blank where the robbery was concerned. Having a gun put to her head had incapacitated all her senses. All she could think about then was dying.

And now somebody thought she was involved. What would he or she or they do to her? If they thought she knew where the jewelry was, how far would they go to get it?

It scared her. Scared her into wishing she could snap her fingers and disappear. Somehow the culprit had found her apartment, and had made it up here to slip a note under her door. Unnoticed.

She wasn't safe. In an instant, the security she had found in the last couple of weeks died.

Just as easily as they had found her, they could, in an instant, kill her.

* * *

Derrick's fingers paused over the laptop's keyboard, an uneasy feeling washing over him. Samona. . . For some reason, his mind was on her. His stomach churned as he thought of her and the hairs on his nape stood on end. Had something happened in the short time since they returned home from their date? Was she okay?

Maybe he just felt bad for lying to her, for making her suffer in public today when he knew she was afraid of being spotted. All this pretending and trying to get close to her was wearing him thin. He was a cop with integrity, and he didn't like being lied to. He didn't like lying, either. He wished there was another way to get at Samona. He wished he could just tell her who he was and force her to confess. But he couldn't do that. Not only would it not work, but it would send Samona running again. This time she would probably leave the state, if not the country.

Derrick's fingers hit the keyboard and a clicking sound filled the silent room. He wrote notes about what happened today, how he felt he was finally making some good progress after a week on assignment. He had called the captain, but Boyle had merely reiterated what he said in his earlier message. Samona needed to be arrested, and soon.

The problem was she had not yet opened up to him. He didn't doubt that she might because she did seem weighted down with her problems. Even tortured. Many people had a breaking point and felt the need to confess their crimes eventually.

Derrick ended his report and closed the laptop. This new development with Milano had him stressed. People like Milano just didn't understand the reality of police investigations; they took time. Suing the department would get him nowhere.

Derrick rose and paced. It was the start of the weekend and he would normally enjoy a competitive squash game with Nick this evening. Yet he was stuck here.

The sooner he wrapped up this case, the sooner he could get back to his life. The only way to do that was to spend more time with Samona. Crossing the living room, Derrick headed to the door.

A blood-curdling scream filled the silence of the old house.

Instantly, Derrick charged down the stairs.

Samona!

CHAPTER NINE

His adrenaline pumping, Derrick charged through her door. A quick glance around the living room told him she was not there. Hearing her soft moans, he rushed into the kitchen. There she stood, shaking a hand over the sink. It took him only a second to realize she was bleeding.

He rushed to her. "Samona. My God, what happened?"

She turned on the faucet and held her injured hand under the flow of water. She winced.

Immediately Derrick took her hand in his and checked the cut. Thankfully, it didn't look very deep. Maybe all the blood scared her. "It's not that bad, Samona. There's just a lot of blood. What happened?"

"I was cutting potatoes . . ."

Derrick glanced at the counter then, noting the cutting board and about three peeled potatoes. The one that was cut in half was sprinkled with blood.

She seemed on the verge of tears. "I'm such a fool."

"Don't say that," Derrick said. "Accidents happen. And as I said, it's not serious."

"But if I'd just been paying attention . . ."

She seemed more upset than she should have been over a simple mishap in the kitchen. Derrick had seen his mother knick herself, burn herself and even cut herself several times. She never got this upset.

Derrick tore off a paper towel from the roll above the sink. He wrapped it around Samona's finger, applying pressure to it. "Do you have any Band-Aids?" he asked.

Samona nodded. "In the bathroom."

"Okay. I'll get one."

Samona watched him rush off, thoughts swirling around in her mind like a tornado. To him, she must seem like a nutcase. First the other night with their dinner, now this. She cut her finger and had totally overreacted and now that he'd come to her rescue, he must think she was so fragile. Maybe she should just tell him about the note, explain to him what had her so on edge.

She was about to do just that as Derrick returned. But as she saw him stroll around the corner, she stopped herself.

No . . . Her eyes flew to his as a thought hit her. It was a disturbing thought, but one that made sense. Who else but Derrick could have placed that note under her door? He had access to her apartment; he knew when she'd been out today . . .

She was such a fool. Here she was spending time with a man she knew nothing about. She only knew his name and where he said he was from. Silently she berated herself for her lack of judgment. Derrick could very easily be behind this. It made sense.

"Give me your hand," Derrick said.

Derrick saw the nervous rise and fall of her chest, the fear in her eyes. In an instant he realized she was afraid of *him*. Why? What had happened in the moments that he'd gone to the bathroom?

"Samona . . ."

"Uh, I want you to leave. I've . . . got this under control. Uh, thanks for coming."

It didn't make sense for her to be afraid of him, certainly not when the gash in her finger was her own fault. Or was it? Derrick stared at her intently, wondering what was wrong, hoping she would confide in him. But she didn't. And he couldn't pressure her, not without blowing his cover.

The look of fear was still in her eyes as he turned and quietly walked away.

In bed that night, sleep eluded him. Samona's eyes haunted him. Something had happened downstairs, something she was afraid to share. He wondered what.

Derrick pondered his reaction to her scream. The moment he'd heard her desperate cry, he had forgotten that she was a criminal he was supposed to investigate. All he had thought of was getting to her, helping her. And then when he'd seen the blood, his heart had pounded wildly in his chest. He'd had the strongest urge to protect her.

Maybe he was just a sucker for a woman in distress. He had wanted to protect Whitney Jordan too. But at least he had been in love with Whitney. He'd had a stake in her safety. She had been his longtime friend and he would not have stood around and let anything happen to her if he could prevent it.

But he hadn't grown up with Samona. He knew her only in one light—as the criminal he was investigating. So why should he care if she seemed in pain? Any pain, stress or other problems she was suffering now were a direct result of her own actions. She had chosen her path and was now dealing with the aftermath of that choice. It was a cruel reality that many didn't learn until they'd gotten involved in criminal activities and been caught. Derrick saw it every day. Young men and women, sometimes even children, learning the devastating results of their actions the hard way. It wasn't uncommon to see a grown man weep.

But none of that affected Derrick the way the look in Samona's eyes had. Her beautiful brown eyes had been filled with fear. That wasn't faked. Something had happened. Something since their date earlier. Something that really scared her.

Maybe he had lost his objectivity. Frustrated, Derrick stood and stretched. He was glad the gym he went to was open twenty-four hours. Nights like these, he needed to relieve his stress.

Samona couldn't sleep. Remembering the night's events, she alternated between being scared and feeling like a fool. Surely, Derrick would think she was crazy. Either that or an emotional basket case. She wasn't sure which was worse.

Partly because of his confused look when he'd come from the washroom, Samona had forced herself to calm down and think. From the time she'd met him earlier this week, Derrick had always been there for her, helping her, trying to make her feel better. She knew now that there was no way Derrick would have put that note under her door. They had spent the day together and had come home at the same time. When would he have had the chance to slip a note under her door? Not only that, but why would he do it? Derrick didn't know her. He was new in town and had no idea who she was.

Every time she had told herself this evening that she didn't know Derrick, that she couldn't trust him, her heart had told her something else. It told her to look at his eyes, the windows to his soul. She saw nothing devious there. Only kindness. Other than that, she got a glimpse of his own pain. He was a good person like she was, trying to work out whatever problems he had in his life.

Rolling over, Samona hugged the pillow, relieved. Derrick could not have been responsible for the note. It didn't make sense.

It was the middle of the day, yet the knocking at the door made her shudder. The note had been delivered in the afternoon. What if the person who'd written the note was at her door now? Sitting on the edge of her bed, Samona's hands literally shook. God, she was so afraid. Afraid because she didn't know whom to fear.

As the knocking persisted, she could hear a faint female voice. Mrs. Jefferson. Of course. Who else would it be? Samona's heart relaxed. If it had been the person who was stalking her, would he have knocked? Samona sensed he'd break the door down in an effort to get at her.

Samona quickly rose, knotting the belt on her terry-cloth robe. It was after noon, but she hadn't dressed. She'd only recently awoken after another sleepless night. Moments later, she opened the door.

"Samantha," Mrs. Jefferson said, clearly relieved. "When you didn't come to the door right away, I was about to call the police. After what Derrick said, I was so worried about you. Thought maybe you were dead inside."

"Derrick . . . said something?"

"He said I should check on you, make sure you were all right. That you didn't seem okay. Guess I overreacted. Looks like you were just sleeping."

"He did?"

"Yes. On his way out just a little while ago. I came up here as soon as I could."

Samona's brain was still registering the fact that Derrick had been concerned enough about her to speak to Mrs. Jefferson. A wave of guilt washed over her. If Derrick had gone to Mrs. Jefferson, he must have realized that for a moment she was afraid of him. She wondered if he'd ever stop surprising her.

"Thanks for coming, Mrs. Jefferson. I'm okay. I just cut myself last night and was a bit upset. Nothing to worry about."

"You sure? Derrick seemed very worried."

Samona nodded, a smile lifting her lips. Derrick took the meaning of nice guy to an extreme. She had never known a man to be that concerned about her—not even Mark.

"Yes. I'm sure." Suddenly she was more sure than she had been for awhile.

"Okay. Go on back and catch up on your beauty sleep."

"Wait," Samona said. She drew in a deep breath. "Did someone come here yesterday looking for me?"

Mrs. Jefferson shook her head. "Not that I can recall. Hmm. Nope."

Samona frowned. "Nobody? Not even a courier? Somebody who told you to leave something for me?"

Her hands on her hips, Mrs. Jefferson was clearly thinking. Again she shook her head. "Nope. Nobody came here yesterday."

Goose bumps broke out on Samona's arms and the back of her neck. She had hoped Mrs. Jefferson could give her some answers. In fact, she had counted on it. For if Mrs. Jefferson hadn't let anybody in to drop a note off for her, then that meant the culprit had somehow gained access to the house without anybody knowing.

"I'll be sure to let you know if somebody drops by today."

"Thanks," Samona said absently. Somehow she knew if that person returned, they wouldn't be knocking on Mrs. Jefferson's door. And this time, they may be breaking down hers.

CHAPTER TEN

The trip to his apartment was uneventful. Partly because he wanted to get Samona off his mind, and partly because he was going crazy with boredom, Derrick had decided to take a trip home this Sunday morning. He'd needed to do something. Being at the apartment in Oak Park, he was tempted to go see Samona, but after the way she had looked at him a couple of nights ago, he knew he had to give her space. The investigation would backfire if she truly became afraid of him.

At his apartment, Derrick had watered his plants—a poinsettia he'd had since Christmas and a big, green and red wide-leafed plant his mother had given him, which he didn't know the name of. Other than that, he'd checked around to make sure that everything was okay. It had been. Even his plants hadn't suffered without him.

He checked his answering machine. There had been one call from his mother. She had wanted to know if he was okay. He had returned her call, but she wasn't at home. Strange, he thought, since this was a Sunday and she always served Sunday dinner at her home. Perhaps there was a luncheon at church, or perhaps Karen and Russell were hosting dinner this afternoon. He didn't know.

When he returned to Oak Park, Derrick took his time climbing the stairs. He was being very quiet, subconsciously listening for any sound in Samona's apartment. He heard none. But that didn't stop him from going to her door.

He should stay away, especially after Friday night and the look of fear she had given him. But how could he stay away, when as a detective with the Chicago PD, it was his duty to investigate her? Whether he liked it or not, he had to spend time with her. He'd spent two days away from her and it was now time to re-establish contact.

He knocked. In less than a minute she opened the door. When she saw him, her face lit up with a big, bright smile. That smile . . . His skin grew warm beneath it and he relaxed. Relaxed, because he suddenly realized that he cared. Cared that she didn't fear him. Even though she should.

"Hi," she said happily.

"What's up?" Derrick asked. She was certainly a different person than she had been two nights ago. Derrick wondered why.

"I want to apologize for the other night," she said. "You always seem to find me at my worst. Believe me, I'm not usually such a downer."

"I didn't think you were."

Samona flashed him a wry smile. "You're too nice of a guy to tell me otherwise."

"Hey, we all have our bad days. I certainly know that."

"Yes, I think you do."

Derrick leaned a shoulder against the door frame. "You seem much better."

"Thanks. I am."

"Good. Because I hate to see a pretty woman cry." His

lips curled ever so slightly in a grin. "If you're up to it, I'd like to invite you to spend the day with me."

Pretty woman. Samona was surprised at her reaction to his words. Until now, she hadn't really known what he thought of her. Now, she couldn't deny the fluttering in her stomach. She suddenly realized that it mattered to her that Derrick thought she was attractive.

"Working," Derrick stressed when she didn't reply. "Since you love working at the beach, why don't we go there?"

Samona was about to say "Okay" when it registered what Derrick had said. She flashed him a puzzled look. "How do you know that?"

"Know what?"

"Know that I love working at the beach?"

Darn. How had he let that slip out? "Uh . . . I just assumed . . . since I found you there the other day with a sketch pad. If you don't want go to the beach that's fine. I just want to see you keep smiling. So if there's somewhere else you would prefer to work, I'm game as long as it makes you happy."

It was too good to be true. Someone putting her needs first. "No. The beach is fine. Or maybe Grant Park. Give me a few minutes to get my stuff."

Grant Park was absolutely beautiful. The sun shone brilliantly in a cloudless blue sky and birds filled the air with song. As it was Sunday, dozens of people were there, walking, in-line skating, playing various sports in the fields or enjoying the free concerts. With the water calm and tempting, many people had taken their boats for a sail.

Derrick, dressed in khaki shorts and a T-shirt, sat on a park bench while Samona sat on the colorful quilt blanket she had brought. Derrick was busy writing in a notebook and Samona was busy sketching. The two had been working in companionable silence for more than ninety minutes.

Derrick stood and stretched, the muscles in his almond-colored legs growing taut. Samona couldn't help looking at him. He was a beautiful creature. Strong. Sexy. *Nice.* She'd always been a sucker for nice guys.

Sitting down, Derrick threw his head back, covering his face with his notebook.

"Don't," Samona said. "I was almost finished."

"Don't what?"

"Don't cover your face. I need to see you to sketch you."

Derrick lifted his head and raised an eyebrow curiously. "You're sketching me?"

Samona shifted on the blanket, repositioning the sketch pad in her lap. "Yes, Derrick. I said don't move."

Because she told him not to move, Derrick chuckled and ran a hand over his face.

"Hey," Samona chastised. "I warned you. If you want to end up looking like Frankenstein. . ."

"Okay." Derrick tried to sit still. No one had ever sketched him before, and he felt self-conscious. He wondered if Samona liked what she saw.

"I should never have told you that I was sketching you. Now you've gotten all stiff. Just relax."

Derrick made a conscious effort to relax. "Give me a second." He lolled his head back and rolled his shoulders. After several seconds, he sat up straight. "All right. I'm relaxed."

Samona giggled watching Derrick. She didn't know what it was about him, but he always made her smile. Maybe he had been a class clown growing up. Whatever his special ability was, she loved it.

"You can still write if you like. You know, pretend I'm not really sketching you. I'm almost finished."

"Naw. I'm enjoying the view. Not every day is as perfect as this one."

Samona wasn't sure if he was talking about the view of the water, of the activity in Grant Park or of her. But his eyes were on her as he said the words, and her pulse pounded in her ears with anticipation.

After a moment, Derrick looked away. It took Samona several seconds to catch her breath. Whoa, that had been an intense moment. Was Derrick trying to send her a message?

Silence fell between them and Samona continued to sketch and smudge to accurately re-create the grooves and angles of Derrick's face. And his dimples. She couldn't forget those incredibly sexy dimples.

Finally, after several minutes she was finished. "Ta da." She presented him the pad in a grand style. "Here you go."

Derrick reached for the pad, his lips pursed in thought. As he scrutinized the picture, his eyes narrowed.

Samona shifted on her feet, then swallowed. She fiddled with her floppy hat, wanting to take it off but didn't dare. It was only a casual sketch, an impromptu thing she'd decided to do just because, but she was suddenly nervous. Nervous that Derrick wouldn't like it. Holding her breath, she waited.

"This is good."

Samona released a long, slow breath. "Really? You really like it?"

"Yeah," Derrick said, nodding. "It's excellent."

Samona smiled. That meant a lot. Maybe more than it should. "I'm glad you like it."

His eyes seem to dance as he looked at her. Again, Samona felt the tension of his heated gaze. "You are one talented lady."

"Thank you." She folded then unfolded her hands in a nervous gesture. "You can have it—if you like."

"I like." She seemed to beam because of his comment, and strangely, it made Derrick happy to see her happy.

His eyes moved from her to the picture. He hadn't lied. He was genuinely impressed. Samona had captured him accurately, right down to the small mole in the center of his chin.

Samona returned to her blanket, sat down, then crossed her legs. It was a simple movement, hardly seductive, but Derrick noticed. Noticed in the way that a man notices a beautiful woman. Noticed her beautiful, slim, nicely shaped legs, her cute butt beneath the pair of tan shorts. Her, smooth caramel skin. Her small waist, her small breasts. He liked looking at her.

Seemingly fidgety, Samona uncrossed her legs and stretched them out on the blanket. She cast a sly look at him over her shoulder, and Derrick wondered if she was silently inviting him to join her. Regardless, he felt compelled to do just that. Closing his notebook, he dropped it onto the grass then slid onto the blanket beside her.

"I think it's time for a break," Derrick announced.

"I agree." When Derrick stretched out beside her, Samona couldn't help giving him the once over. Her eyes roamed the length of his body, his wide chest, his strong arms beneath his cotton shirt, his thighs. Her gaze fell to his legs, similar to hers in complexion, then rested on the scar that began at his knee and stretched to his mid-calf. She didn't have to ask to know that the scar had been obtained painfully. But she asked anyway, "How did that happen?"

"My scar, you mean?"

Samona nodded.

Derrick had seen her eyes linger on his legs and wasn't surprised when she asked him about the scar. This was his chance, his opportunity to "open up" to her in hopes that she would trust him, then open up to him as well. He now felt uneasy at the thought of lying to her and said, "I'm not sure you want to know."

"I do."

Derrick drew in a long, slow, steady breath and released it in a rush. His voice was a mere whisper when he said, "Families can be cruel."

Samona felt the overwhelming urge to reach out and stroke Derrick's face. His eyes were a mixture of many emotions, and she knew he was in pain. She wanted to say something to him, but couldn't. She sensed what he had gone through was horrible and her words would be meaningless. The only thing she could do for him was listen. "If you want to talk . . ."

Reaching for a blade of grass, Derrick snatched it and shredded it. Then he sighed, a long, sad sound. "My father."

Samona's heart ached for him. She had been right. They did have something in common—pain in their families. She waited, giving him the time he needed.

After several seconds, he spoke again. She wished he would look at her but his eyes remained firmly on a spot on the blanket. "My father used to beat my mother. When I tried to stop him, he would beat me. I got the scar one of those times. He was beating my mother really bad, and I ran at him, pounding my small fists on his body as hard as I could. He grabbed me and threw me. I flew in the air and landed on the glass coffee table. It broke and sliced my leg."

"Oh my God." Samona threw a hand to her mouth.

"I was . . . maybe seven. I can't remember." Derrick's voice was void of emotion, but Samona knew his heart ached. Ached the way hers did every time she talked to Evelyn or thought of her sister's betrayal.

Sitting, silently watching him, Samona didn't know what to say. What could she say? After a long moment, Derrick continued.

"The beatings went on for years. It was always the same— my father drunk, angry or just plain hateful. Any little thing set him off. My mother and I—we were so afraid of him." Derrick paused, bit his lip. "I'd made a vow to protect my mother, but I failed."

Samona's stomach lurched painfully. "Did—your mother—" How did you ask somebody about something so painful?

"She lost an eye. It could have been worse—she could have lost her life. But I should have protected her."

Samona didn't think. She acted. Her hand reached out and gently rubbed Derrick's arm. "Derrick, don't blame yourself. You were only a child."

"I should have called the police. That was the least I could do. But I was too afraid—afraid that he would get so angry he would kill my mother."

Samona's fingers trailed upwards on Derrick's arm and found his face. She framed it. "You did the best you could."

Derrick moved away from her touch. Her hand lingered in the air, then after a moment, feeling somewhat awkward, Samona pulled her hand back and placed it on her chest.

"I should have done better."

"No," Samona said softly. "Don't say that, Derrick. There are so many things in life that we just can't control. I know that. I learned that the hard way." Just remembering her own pain caused her voice to break. "I . . . lost my parents. I know it's not the same as what you went through, but the pain was just as intense. And the guilt."

Derrick looked at her then, gazing intently into her eyes. "Guilt? Why?"

"Because," Samona said quickly, then stopped. She seemed to be searching for the right words to say. "Because I should have been there for them. I didn't spend enough time with them. If I hadn't been running from my sister and my problems like a spoiled child, I would've been there for my parents."

He captured an ebony wisp of her hair and twirled it around a finger. "Why were your running?"

"Because I had my share of problems with my sister. But I should never have let that take me away from my parents. Even if I couldn't deal with what my sister had done, I didn't have to leave town. I didn't even go to see them that last Christmas because I'd wanted to avoid my sister. And then they died. . . ." Samona's voice trailed off.

She seemed so overwhelmed by her guilt and pain that Derrick felt for her. And he felt like a jerk. His story had been fiction; hers was the truth. "Don't," he said. "From what you just said I'm sure you had your reasons for leaving. I'm sure your parents understood that as well. It won't do any good to beat yourself up now. I know it's a cliché, but you can't turn back the clock. And you have to ask yourself, would your parents want you to be sitting here grieving like this, blaming yourself for something you couldn't control?"

Samona wiped her tears. Derrick was right. Her parents knew she loved them, always would. Wherever they were now, she was sure they knew that. But still, every time she thought about how they had died without her seeing them one last time, the guilt overwhelmed her.

"I guess you're right," she said softly.

"But there's more, isn't there?" Derrick asked. "Something that's going on now—more than what happened with your parents?" He was pushing, and he wondered if Samona would take the bait and tell him what he wanted to know. Wondered if he really wanted her to. For if she did, he would have to arrest her. Derrick swallowed, but the lump in his throat wouldn't go away. He felt like a heel, conning her.

"Yeah, there's more."

He didn't breathe.

"I guess I just feel very alone sometimes. I have nobody to turn to, to share my problems with. My parents are gone, and my sister and I don't talk. . . ."

"Why not?" Derrick asked gently.

"That's a very long story."

"What about boyfriends? Or a former boyfriend you're still close to?"

Samona shook her head. "No. Any man I have been close to has betrayed me."

Derrick ignored the shame overwhelming him and continued. "Really? I find that hard to believe."

"It's true. I don't know why." Her petite shoulders rose and fell. "Maybe I'm not special enough."

She couldn't be a criminal, Derrick decided. It was impossible. As much as his brain told him she was involved in the jewelry store robbery and murder, his heart told him it wasn't true. There was just something about her, something inherently good. Something too vulnerable, too sweet. He could pry, ask her more about this boyfriend who had betrayed her. He should. But part of him didn't want to know.

"You're very special." Much to his surprise, he edged closer to her and slipped an arm around her waist. He felt her stiffen at his touch and that should have stopped him, but it didn't. He couldn't help himself. Pulling her close, he brought his face near hers. Her eyes held his for several moments, startled, questioning eyes. He could get lost in those eyes. For a moment, he was.

As he brought his lips slowly down onto hers, he told himself that this was just part of the plan to get to know her, to get her to trust him. But his heart told him that was a lie.

Her mouth was soft and sweet. Like an exotic flower. He ran his lips over hers ever so gently, simply enjoying. The action seemed almost foreign to him in its arousing effect and he realized just how long it had been since he had last kissed a woman. Pressing his hand against her back, pulling her closer, he parted his lips and began to kiss her. Softly.

Samona sighed and her eyes fluttered shut. Derrick's lips were like a feather, softly touching hers, teasing her. A tingling sensation spiraled from her stomach outward to her skin, down her arms and legs to her fingertips and to her toes. The wonderful feeling took over her entire body. She couldn't remember ever feeling this reaction to Mark when he'd kissed her, and she had been in love with him. Or so she had thought.

She felt safe in Derrick's arms. Like maybe her world wasn't falling apart. As he pulled her closer, she arched into his embrace. She slipped an arm around his back as he deepened the kiss. His tongue was warm, persistent, thrilling. If this was a dream, she didn't want to wake up.

Slowly his tongue mated with hers, dancing together as though they always had. He should stop. Pull away. Right now. End the kiss. But he didn't want to. Couldn't. Not when it felt so good.

Finally, Samona placed a hand on his chest and gently eased him away, breaking the kiss. She was so beautiful, her lips glistening, her eyelids closed. Derrick's mouth immediately felt cold. He looked down at her as she slowly opened her eyes. In a breathless whisper, she asked, "Why'd you do that?"

The attraction he was feeling for her made no sense. Sitting up, Derrick rested his elbows on his knees. "I don't know."

Samona's stomach fluttered. She had hoped for a different answer, but sensed that Derrick was as confused and shocked by the kiss as she was. Bringing a hand to her lips, Samona trailed a finger along the outline of her mouth.

It was a wonderful kiss. Though startled when Derrick had drawn her close, Samona had to admit that she had been hoping he would kiss her all day. Hoping, despite the fact that she didn't want to get close to another man. Her life was too screwed up for any relationship.

But God help her, if Derrick were to take her in his arms again, she would let him. Let him kiss her. Let him take her to a place where there were no worries.

Derrick spoke then, ending the fantasy. "It's been a long day. I think we should go."

CHAPTER ELEVEN

Later that evening, Samona still remembered Derrick's kiss as she sat on her living room sofa, staring. Staring, but seeing nothing.

His kiss. *Him*. Derrick had made her feel so alive, so incredibly desirable for the first time in a very long time. That was something she'd needed, had wanted, but hadn't known Derrick could give that to her until he'd actually placed his sensuous lips on hers. Now, her lips still tingled with electricity. . . .

The shrill ring of the telephone drew Samona from her musing. She welcomed the distraction because Derrick had monopolized her thoughts. Hopping off the sofa, she hurried across the warm hardwood floor to the telephone stand. She answered it on the third ring. "Hello."

"Samona . . . hi."

Samona froze, her hand gripping the receiver. "Evelyn."

"How are you, Samona?"

"Didn't we go through this a couple of days ago? I think we said all we needed to say then."

"Please don't hang up."

"Fine. Make it quick."

"Okay. I'm going to be in Chicago tomorrow. I'll be there for a three-day business trip. I was hoping . . . maybe we could get together."

Samona's stomach clenched. "Why?"

"Because we haven't seen each other for more than two years."

"So why start now?" She sounded harsh, like she didn't care. But it was the only way. It was the only way to try to avoid the painful memories of her sister's betrayal.

There was a short, tension-filled pause before Evelyn said, "We have a lot of things to work out, Samona, but . . . I think we can. We need to. You're the only family I have left."

"Aren't things going well with Mark?" Samona was not able to hide the sarcasm in her voice.

"Mark is fine. I'm fine."

"See . . ." Samona's throat was suddenly tight, aching with suppressed emotion. "You have your family right there in Dallas. You don't need me. You never did."

Evelyn must have heard the pain in her voice for she said, "Samona, I didn't call to hurt you."

Samona muttered, "You could have fooled me."

"I'm trying to make an effort. Maybe it is a little too late, but I'm hoping that you'll give me a chance. We've let this go on way too long."

"We? You're the one who wasn't happy unless you were hurting me. Don't you put this on me—"

"You're right. I'm sorry. *I've* let this go on too long. Samona, I want to try to make amends. . . ."

Samona didn't know what to believe. Her sister actually sounded sincere. But she was still hurting. Maybe always would when she thought of what her sister had done.

Samona frowned into the receiver, fighting to keep the tears at bay. Maybe her sister was right. Maybe enough

3 QUICK STEPS
TO RECEIVE YOUR "THANK YOU" GIFT
FROM THE EDITOR

Send back this card and you'll receive 4 Arabesque novels!
These books have a combined cover price of $20.00 or more,
but they are yours to keep for a mere $1.99.

There's no catch. You're under no obligation to buy anything.
We charge only $1.99 for the books (plus $1.50 for shipping
and handling). And you don't have to make any minimum
number of purchases—not even one!

We hope that after receiving your books you'll want to
remain an Arabesque subscriber. But the choice is yours to
continue or cancel, anytime at all! So why not take us up on
our invitation to receive 4 Arabesque Romance Novels, with
no risk of any kind. You'll be glad you did!

THE EDITOR'S "THANK YOU" GIFT INCLUDES:
4 books delivered for only $1.99 (plus $1.50 for shipping and handling)

A FREE newsletter, Arabesque Romance News, filled with author
interviews, book previews, special offers, BET "Buy The Book"
information, and more!

No risks or obligations. You're free to cancel whenever you wish . . .
with no questions asked

BOOK CERTIFICATE

Yes! Please send me 4 Arabesque books for $1.99 (+ $1.50 for shipping &
handling). I understand I am under no obligation to purchase any books, as
explained on the back of this card.

Name _____

Address_____ Apt. _____

City_____ State_____ Zip_____

Telephone ( ) _____

Signature _____

Offer limited to one per household and not valid to current subscribers. All orders subject
to approval. Terms, offer, & price subject to change.

Thank you!

AC0499

Accepting the four introductory books for $1.99 (+ $1.50 for shipping & handling places you under no obligation to buy anything. You may keep the books and return the shipping statement marked "cancel". If you do not cancel, about a month later we will send 4 additional Arabesque novels, and bill you a preferred subscriber's price of just $4.00 per title (plus a small shipping and handling fee). That's $16.00 for all 4 books for a savings of 25% off the publisher's price. You may cancel at any time, but if you choose to continue, every month we'll send you 4 more books, which you may either purchase at the preferred discount price. . . or return to us and cancel your subscription.

THE ARABESQUE ROMANCE CLUB
c/o ZEBRA HOME SUBSCRIPTION SERVICE, INC.
120 BRIGHTON ROAD
P.O. BOX 5214
CLIFTON, NEW JERSEY 07015-5214

AFFIX
STAMP
HERE

time had passed and it was time to try and save their relationship. Giving in, Samona asked, "What time are you getting in tomorrow?"

Evelyn gave Samona all the details of her stay in Chicago, and Samona scribbled the information onto the notepad beside the phone. "Okay. I'll see if I can spare some time."

"I hope you can. I'd really like to see you."

"We'll see." Samona wiped a sweaty hand on her shorts. "I'm not making any promises."

"I understand."

Samona was about to hang up when she heard her sister call her name. Her heart pounded painfully in her chest. "Yes, Evelyn?"

Evelyn said softly, "Thanks."

Samona held the small notepad to her chest long after she had hung up the phone. Inhaling deep breaths did not ease the ache in her heart. Twice in a week Evelyn had called her when they hadn't spoken more than twice in two years.

If only it were easy to just get her sister out of her life, to forget her. But as this was a time in her life when she particularly felt the need to talk to someone, she couldn't help wishing she and Evelyn were close. She was the only family she had left.

She remembered the horrible accident in Dallas two years ago. Her parents hadn't known what hit them when a tractor trailer crossed the center line and collided with their car head-on.

Two years, and still the pain was fresh, raw. Never could Samona think of the accident without getting emotional. Her parents had been cheated. She had been cheated. And what made it worse for her to deal with was the fact that she hadn't seen her parents in more than a year because she'd stayed away from Dallas. She'd stayed away from Evelyn.

How could she get over all this, at least enough to forgive her sister? It wasn't Evelyn's fault, but Samona did partially blame her. If Evelyn hadn't stolen then married her boyfriend, Samona would never have left Dallas for Chicago. She would have spent more time with her parents before they died.

Samona sighed. Her parents were gone, and nothing would bring them back. But she still had a sister. Maybe it was time to make an effort at salvaging their relationship.

Tempting. Samona was too tempting.

Derrick closed his eyes as he lay on the well-worn living-room sofa. He tightened his fingers around the black beanbag in his hand, then relaxed them, continuing that routine for several minutes as thoughts whirled in his mind. Thoughts of Samona.

What he couldn't understand was why he had kissed her. Of all the stupid things to do, that had to be the worst.

Derrick squeezed the beanbag as hard as he could, but it didn't relieve the tension in his gut. He'd blown it, gotten too close to a suspect. How on earth had he lost his objectivity?

Opening his eyes, Derrick stared at the ceiling. The crazy part was, he didn't really regret doing it, even though he should. His brain told him that he was a fool but he couldn't forget the feeling of Samona's soft lips beneath his, slowly opening, accepting his tongue. Even now, he felt a rush remembering.

What was happening to him? He was a cop, and except for that one time, he always thought with his head, not his emotions. How had he let himself get so attracted to Samona? He didn't have an answer. He only knew that in some way he was attracted to her. As much as he wanted to, he couldn't deny that.

It was hard to accept—whatever this attraction was. He'd only felt such a strong attraction for one woman before: Whitney Jordan.

Though he was over Whitney, he hadn't expected to feel something for anyone else in a long time. Maybe never. Now, his feelings toward Samona were unwanted and frustrated him. Frustrated him because he shouldn't feel anything for her. She was a criminal.

Good God, what was wrong with him?

Derrick got up and moved around the apartment, trying to get the kiss he and Samona had shared off his mind. But he couldn't. The taste of her sweet lips, the velvety soft feel of them, were constantly on his mind.

Finally he found himself at the phone in his bedroom. Picking up the receiver, he dialed Whitney's number. He didn't know why, other than the attraction he felt for Samona seemed in some strange way like a betrayal to Whitney, after all he'd felt for her.

When the butler answered, Derrick identified himself and asked for Whitney. Several seconds later, she came to the phone.

"Derrick!" she squealed. "How are you?"

Hearing Whitney's voice brought a smile to his face. A smile like the kind his own sister brought out in him. "I'm cool. How's my favorite girl?"

"Exhausted. Reanna and Marcus have me running around like a chicken with my head cut off. You know how it is—when one cries, the other cries. Now they're teething at the same time. . . ."

"No, I don't know how it is, but I'll take your word for it."

Whitney laughed. "Sometimes I don't know if I'm coming or going. Having twins isn't easy."

"But it sounds like you're loving every minute of it."

"You know it."

"So where are they now?"

"Sleeping. Thank God."

Derrick said, "How is Javar?"

"He's great. Tired, but great."

Derrick could hear the smile in her voice and that gave him a deep sense of satisfaction. He wondered if he would ever have made her as happy as Javar made her. He doubted it.

"We've got to hook up sometime," he said. "I haven't seen those kids in so long." A year and a half ago, he would not have been able to picture himself as a welcome guest at Javar's house. Now, he was exactly that. It was amazing how things could change given time.

"And they've grown so much. I swear, it seems like only yesterday they were these tiny babies in my arms. Seven months later, my mother keeps asking me what I'm feeding them!"

Derrick chuckled. "Motherhood certainly suits you. I don't think I've ever known you to be happier than you are now."

"I don't think I have been. Javar and I finally have our lives back on track and everything is working out the way it was meant to be." She sighed, happily. "Well, enough about me. What's up with you?"

"Oh, the same old same old. Work and more work."

"When are you going to find some time to play?" Whitney asked. "You're too nice to let life pass you by without having any fun."

"I'm having . . . fun. Work is entertaining."

"Yeah right."

Derrick twirled the phone's cord around his hand. "One of these days, Whitney, I'll be as happy as you."

"Okay. What's wrong?"

"What makes you think something is wrong?"

"Because I've only known you since I was a kid. Something's up, Derrick. What is it?"

Derrick dragged his bottom lip into his mouth, wondering how much he should tell Whitney. He blew out a ragged breath. "It's a case I'm working on."

"What kind of case?"

"Undercover."

"Hmm . . . Let me guess—it involves a woman."

Derrick's mouth fell open. How on earth had she figured that out? "Why do you say that?"

"Because the only time I have to drag information out of you is when a woman is involved. Is she a partner in crime?"

"Not exactly."

Whitney paused. "Okay. Is she someone special, or is she like all the other women you've dated in the past—a passing fancy?"

"Hey," Derrick said. "What are you trying to say? That I'm some type of player?"

"No," Whitney replied. "But you certainly are a hard man to please."

"That's because all the good women are taken." He shouldn't have said that, but couldn't take back the words.

"Hmm," was all Whitney said. He was certain she knew the meaning behind his words, yet she said nothing. He was glad. He didn't want to make her uncomfortable. He was happy for her. Despite the feelings he'd had for her in the past, he knew that Javar was the right man for her. Javar was the man who could give her what she needed, wanted. Not him.

"I'm sure there are a few good women out there," she continued. "And if I'm right, you didn't really call to say hi, but to talk because you're confused. Maybe you're feeling something for someone you didn't expect to feel. Am I right?"

"W—well, kind of . . ." Derrick sputtered, shocked at how perceptive Whitney was.

"Then it seems to me like you've finally found someone you're interested in."

Whitney was too smart, Derrick thought as he shook his head, a crooked grin playing on his lips. He wanted to deny her allegation, but the words wouldn't come. He finally said, "It's a difficult situation."

"Work it out."

"Easier said than done, Whitney." Especially in this case. The direction of his thoughts startled him. Without thinking, he had basically admitted that he did want things to work out with Samona.

"But you're thinking about it. Oh, I'm so happy for you. This is serious."

"Don't start planning my wedding yet."

"I'd just better be the first one you invite."

Derrick laughed. Javar was a lucky man. "If and when that time comes, you'll be the first to know."

When Samona heard the soft knocking on the door, her heart leaped to her throat. An image of Derrick smiling at her, his cute dimples winking at her, flashed in her mind. Why she couldn't get him off her mind she didn't know.

She sprang from the couch. A rose-colored silk nightie and matching robe reached her mid-thigh. It had been ages since she'd had the desire to put something sexy like this on, and now she knew she'd wanted to look sexy for Derrick in case he came by.

She was losing her mind.

At the door, she reached for the knob. Her fingers froze on the handle as she remembered two days ago. Remembered the note.

"Who is it?" she called instead.

"It's Derrick."

Just the sexy way he said his name made her pulse race. Slowly, she opened the door.

For a moment, Derrick merely stared at her, his eyes roaming her body from head to toe. His eyes seared her skin, making her hot. She loved the way he looked at her.

"I'm sorry, Samona," he finally said. "I didn't mean to disturb you."

"You're not disturbing me." *I'm glad you're here,* she thought.

"You look ready for bed." Maybe she was imagining it, but his voice sounded raspy. Because of her?

"No." She angled her head to the right, letting wisps of hair fall over her face. "Not yet."

Derrick's eyes caught the movement and she saw interest flash in their depths. He cleared his throat, folded his arms over his chest, then spoke. "I don't have your phone number, so I couldn't call."

"That's okay. So, what's on your mind?"

Holding her gaze, he said, "If I tell you that, I think I might be arrested."

Every inch of her responded to his words, knowing they were meant for her. Her nipples tightened, her pulse throbbed, her body thrummed with desire. He was attracted to her, like she was to him.

"Okay, time to get serious." He flashed one of his charming smiles and Samona wished he would take her in his arms and kiss her again. "I just thought I'd drop by to say that I really enjoyed today. And I was hoping you'd like to spend the day with me tomorrow."

Samona felt a niggling disappointment, but knew that Derrick was right not to take her up on the silent offer she was making. It was too soon to go too far in their relationship. They needed to take things slowly.

She took a moment to consider his proposal, not wanting to seem too anxious. "Sure. Why not?"

"Great. I can't wait."

"Great. I can't wait."

Good grief, what had he been thinking? Lying in bed, his hands behind his head, Derrick wondered what on earth had gotten into him.

When he had gone to Samona's apartment, he had planned to extend an invitation to spend more time with her. After all, that was what he was being paid to do. He hadn't planned to sound so excited about it.

But then, he hadn't expected to see her in that sexy silky number. She had been silently seducing him with every movement of her eyes, every gesture she made, every soft-spoken word. Somehow, he had respectfully declined.

For now. With his foolish "I can't wait" statement, Samona would surely be expecting something more in this relationship.

Maybe he should call the captain and tell him that he could no longer continue with this assignment. That he had lost his objectivity. That for some reason, around Samona he seemed to lose all reason.

"Yeah right, Lawson," Derrick said aloud. He could imagine Captain Boyle's "delight" at that news.

No, Derrick would continue with the assignment. He would push all thoughts of the tempting Samona aside and try to remember his reason for being here in this old house in Oak Park in the first place.

But deep in his heart, Derrick wondered if that was possible any longer.

CHAPTER TWELVE

Samona sat cross-legged on the quilt, staring at the spectacular flower gardens in the distance. They were a dazzling array of colors—reds, whites, oranges, violets, pinks, blues. She should paint them, and capture the beautiful, sparkling blue water in the distance behind them. She would, one day, but not today.

She adjusted the rim of her floppy cotton hat to protect her eyes from the glare of the sun, and as always, to keep her identity adequately hidden. She was surprised at the number of people here. Despite it being a Monday, several people strolled the fabulous gardens and lawn, enjoying Grant Park. People must have called in sick to work, Samona thought.

She frowned. Not even she felt like working. The sketch pad in her lap was blank. Today, she didn't feel like sketching. Maybe finger painting, sponge painting or something fun like that. It felt like one of those "Crazy Days" as she would tell her students on those occasions when she felt like doing something different with her class. On Crazy

Days, the students got to be creative in their own way, doing their own thing however they wanted. Later, if they wanted to, they could share their work with the class.

Her students . . . Crazy Days . . . Sighing, Samona closed her eyes.

"All right," Derrick announced. "What do you say we take a break from work and have some fun."

"Work?" Samona chuckled sarcastically. "What work? I've gotten nothing done today."

Derrick grinned sheepishly. "Neither have I."

"It must be the weather," Samona said. Or the fact that she couldn't forget his kiss and couldn't stop wishing he'd kiss her again. His kiss was ever present on her mind and had made her lose all interest in her art.

"Must be," Derrick agreed.

Samona turned, looking out at the lake, anything to try to gain control of her wayward thoughts. It was another beautiful June day. Though still officially spring, it felt like summer. But at least the heat was offset by the cool breeze coming off the water.

"You said something about fun?" Samona faced Derrick. She wondered what kind of fun he had in mind.

"Mmm hmm."

"Well . . . ?" He certainly knew how to keep a woman in suspense.

"How about we go to the marina and see if we can rent a boat. Or pay someone to take us out on theirs. I'd love to go for a sail."

A boat . . . Roger. For a moment, Samona forgot to breathe. She tried to smile, to disguise her reaction, but couldn't.

Derrick flashed her a worried look. "You don't like that idea?"

"It's just that . . . I–I know someone who died on a boat recently . . ."

"Taking foot out of mouth." Jokingly, Derrick pretended to wrestle with his foot.

Samona's shoulders sagged with relief. With one silly smile, Derrick had succeeded in easing the tension. He knew just what to do to make her feel better.

She stared at him for a moment. He was hard to figure out. One minute, he seemed depressed because of his own problems. The next, he seemed like he didn't have a care in the world.

Derrick caught her staring. "What? Something on my face?"

"No."

"Then what?"

"You're just . . . so interesting."

His eyes narrowed. "Interesting good, or interesting bad?"

"Good. You," she paused, cast her eyes downward, "make me laugh."

"A pretty woman like you should laugh more."

Pretty . . . As Samona stared at Derrick, she felt a tingling sensation spread through her stomach. She wanted to kiss him again. God help her.

Derrick clapped his hands together, breaking the moment. "Any other ideas?"

"We could get a hot dog."

Derrick made a face. "I don't eat that stuff."

Samona nodded, realizing how silly that suggestion was. Derrick was a health-conscious man. "Of course."

"How about an ice-cream cone?"

Samona jumped to her feet. "You're on."

Marie retreated down the steps and hustled to the car. She opened the passenger side door and slipped inside. She said to Alex in a whisper, "She's not home. Nobody is."

Framing her face, Alex kissed Marie long and hard. He was such a good kisser. That was one of the things she loved about him.

Breaking the kiss, he looked into her eyes. For the first time in weeks, he looked interested in her again, like he truly loved her. He winked, then said, "Let's do this."

Samona couldn't remember laughing so much in recent months. For two hours, she had forgotten she'd had a care in the world. She and Derrick had toured Grant Park extensively, walking along the paths to the Petrillo Music Shell where free summer concerts were held, to the Adler Planetarium and then the Field Museum of Natural History. They had strolled around Buckingham Fountain, a massive, circular fountain with many spouts. Derrick had even held her waist as she dipped a foot into the water, making sure she didn't fall. Later, they played an impromptu game of soccer with a crumpled paper ball on the grass. She was like a carefree child, frolicking and laughing.

Now, they were both outside her door, laughing once again. Laughing at something silly—she couldn't even remember what.

When the laughing died, their eyes met and held. It was the awkward moment after a date when neither knew what to say. It was a moment of anticipation. Would he kiss her? Would he not?

When he reached out and stroked her face, Samona knew then that he would. He made her feel so wonderful. So wanted. So distanced from her troubles.

As he lowered his head toward hers, the energy sizzled between them and it seemed like it took forever for their lips to meet. Finally, Derrick's delicious mouth covered hers. Having waited for this moment all day, Samona closed her eyes and surrendered to the kiss. She whimpered faintly, slipped her hands around Derrick's back. Trailed her fingers over his muscles. Squeezed, probed. Pressed her body closer to his.

Derrick moaned when she pressed her breasts against his chest. It was a deep moan, and seemed to rumble from his chest to hers. Never had she felt such need, the need to be close to another human being. To a man. To Derrick.

Derrick broke the kiss and looked at her. His hazel eyes had darkened with desire. His lips were wet and so seductive. His hand was still on her face, gently stroking her skin, exciting her. Samona covered his hand with hers, brought her lips to his fingers and kissed his rough skin.

"Samona . . ." His voice was a velvety rasp.

"Yes?" She looked at him with longing. What she was feeling now was so strong and she wanted to know that he felt it too.

"I . . . I've . . . I . . ." He lowered his head and kissed her again.

It was a kiss that ignited a fire in her belly. She had been hesitating at the door because she wasn't sure, but now she knew what to do. She knew what she wanted. Breaking the kiss, she said, "Derrick . . . let's go inside."

Derrick merely nodded. Turning, Samona found her key and unlocked her door as quickly as she could. She opened it and stepped inside.

In an instant, the excitement, the longing she had felt only a moment ago, died. She gasped. Threw a hand to her chest as she looked around her apartment in horror.

"Oh my God!"

CHAPTER THIRTEEN

Derrick brushed past Samona, moving into the apartment slowly as she stood behind him paralyzed with fear. "What the hell?" he asked.

Someone had broken into her apartment. As she stepped cautiously into the living room, Samona's eyes registered the mess, saw the overturned chairs, the trashed artwork, papers all over the floor. Yet her heart didn't want to believe it was true. Who would've done this to her?

"Samona, do you have any idea who would have done this?"

Derrick was gripping her shoulders, looking into her face, but Samona hardly noticed. Her body was shaking.

"Samona?"

Her head moved slightly. It seemed that was all she could do. Derrick wasn't sure if her reply was a yes or a no. He only knew that she needed him. Wrapping her in his arms, he held her tight, offering comfort. She was so afraid, she trembled. He was afraid for her.

Somebody wanted to hurt her. He wished he could do more for her, protect her from the danger. Because he sensed she needed protection. According to her, she had nobody else.

He said, "Think, Samona. Think hard. Is there any-one—"

"No." She pulled out of his embrace and faced him. She looked both confused and terrified at the same time. Derrick had seen that expression in his role as police officer many times. When he told someone that a loved one had been badly injured or killed in an accident. When he informed someone of a family member's arrest. Or murder. Or any number of other things.

"Just stay here a moment," Derrick said. "I'm going to check out the rest of your apartment. I'll be right back." When she didn't reply, Derrick shook her gently. "Samona . . . ?"

Her head bobbed up and down in jerky movements. Her mouth was open but the only sound that escaped was wheezing as she struggled to breathe. Her eyes bulging, she clawed at her throat.

"Breathe, Samona." She was having a panic attack. He'd recognize one anywhere.

"I'm o–k–kay."

"No, you're not." He held her shoulders firmly. "Breathe, Samona. Concentrate. In. Out. C'mon, you can do it." As she followed his instructions, the wheezing slowed and died but it still seemed like it was an effort for her to breathe. "That's it. You're doing real good. Just keep breathing. I'm going to get you some water." Derrick ran to the kitchen and in seconds returned with a glass of water. "Drink this."

He placed the glass at her mouth, but Samona jerked her head away. "It's okay, Samona. I'm here with you and it's going to be okay."

She seemed to grow calmer at his words, and finally accepted the glass. She took a large gulp and choked.

"Not so much," Derrick told her. He rubbed her back until the coughing stopped.

"No. . .no water."

"You're sure?"

She nodded.

Her breathing was now regular, but she still seemed terrified. Derrick didn't know what to do to help her. He wondered if she always got panic attacks. "Will you be okay for a few minutes? I want to look around."

"O–kay."

For a moment, Derrick felt guilty. Guilty for leaving her there in the living room so distraught. But he was a cop. He knew what to look for and right now, had a job to do. Still, he couldn't forget the look in her eyes. That desolate, frightened look.

How had he gotten to the point where he cared so much? Cared for a woman who was accused of a heinous crime?

Ignoring that thought, Derrick headed to her bedroom. It was the same as the living room. The mattresses were thrown from the bed, drawers and clothes littered the floor. Amidst the mess, his eyes caught a pile of lacy lingerie, and for an instant, he tried to imagine Samona wearing something sexy for him. Something white and lacy and skimpy. The image disturbed him, and Derrick swallowed.

When he returned to the living room, he righted the sofa and returned the cushions to their rightful place. "Samona, come here. Take a seat."

"The kitchen. Everything."

Derrick took her by the shoulders, noting her skin felt clammy and cold. She jerked when he touched her. All he wanted to do was make her pain go away, but he couldn't.

She didn't protest when he led her to the sofa. When

she was seated, he went to the kitchen. The stove had been moved from the wall, the paper-towel roll was scattered on the floor, the drawers and cupboards were open and their contents dumped. Even the toaster lay on the floor.

Why? Derrick wondered.

Moments later, he returned to the living room and sat beside Samona. He didn't know why her place had been torn apart like this, but he knew she needed to call the police. If she did, he would be a witness and his cover would no doubt be blown. He didn't care. He wanted Samona safe. "You have to call the police."

"No." Samona looked at her folded hands.

"Do you want me to call them for you?"

"No." Her reply was sharp.

"Why not? This is a crime scene. You need to—"

Samona threw her gaze to him and he saw then that her eyes were filled with tears. "I can't . . . You don't understand. . . ."

But he did. She was afraid of the police. He wondered how she would react when she learned the truth about him. Would she hate him? It didn't matter. Her safety came first.

"This is serious," he said. "Somebody obviously wants to hurt you. The police can protect you."

She laughed sarcastically and he thought she would cry. Finally she said, "I'm not going to call the police. Please don't call them for me. I don't want them involved."

"But—"

"I'm not going to change my mind."

Frustrated, Derrick sighed. "Well if you won't let me help you that way, will you at least accept my invitation to stay with me tonight? You can't stay here."

He saw the first sign of relief in her eyes since he had offered her comfort. "Yes. Get me out of here, Derrick."

* * *

She hadn't said much since he'd brought her to his apartment, and now she lay sleeping on his sofa. He watched her from the neighboring arm seat. She lay on her side, her head resting on her arm, her small body curled in the fetal position. Her lips were slightly parted and strands of her onyx hair fell across her face. She was beautiful. She was forbidden. But there was something about her he couldn't resist. Something too tempting.

If they hadn't found her apartment ransacked, he wondered what would have happened when she invited him inside. He certainly wanted to make love to her. Wanted to more strongly than he had wanted anything. But would he have? Would he have broken his vow to the department? As much as he hated discovering Samona's apartment in such a state of turmoil, it had prevented him from making a terrible mistake.

Someone had ransacked her apartment, literally torn her place apart. This certainly added a new element to his investigation. Who had done it and why? He had no doubt it was connected to the robbery. Was it somebody who knew or thought she had the jewelry? And did this have anything to do with the private investigator someone had hired? The questions swirled around in his mind, but he had no answers.

The only thing he knew for sure was that he was glad he was with her when she'd returned home. There to protect her, comfort her the best way he could. The frightened look in her eyes still haunted him. She was so vulnerable, fragile. If she had walked in on her intruder, he shuddered to think what could have happened. She was only five foot four, hardly a match for a strong man with a deadly agenda.

Samona stirred, moaned. Instantly, Derrick moved to

her side. Softly he brushed her hair off her face and looked down at her with wonder. How could a woman who seemed so soft, sweet, fragile, be behind such horrible crimes? But that question fled his mind as he lifted her into his arms. She snuggled her face into his neck and Derrick could only wonder why his body was betraying his mind. It was like he had totally forgotten why he was here, what job he had to do. Instead, his body grew warm in reaction to her need for him.

He was crazy.

He took her to the bedroom and placed her on his bed. She could get a good night's sleep here as opposed to on the sofa.

As he looked down at her sprawled on the blue comforter, his hands were sweating. Suddenly he was nervous. Not only did he need to slip her under the covers, but he needed to disrobe her. Just the thought felt like a violation. A violation because she trusted him when she shouldn't.

His mouth went dry and he closed his eyes. God, how could he do this? What if she awoke while he was slipping off her shorts? As a cop, he knew the possible ramifications. She could charge him with sexual assault, claim he had taken advantage of her. But as a man . . . No. He couldn't touch her. Instead, he took a blanket from the closet and covered her.

He was almost out the bedroom door when she called him. Her voice sounded soft and sultry, like she was calling to her lover. His skin prickled with excitement and heat pooled in his groin. If things were different . . .

"Yes?" He was surprised at the huskiness of his voice.

"I know you don't understand all this, Derrick, and you must think I'm crazy."

The urge to go to her, to take her in his arms was so strong, it was tangible. She looked so incredibly sexy with her slightly messy hair, her sleepy eyes. "No," he managed to say. "I don't think you're crazy."

Her lips curled into a grin. "Well, I just want to thank you. For understanding. And for being there."

"No problem."

"Good night."

"Night."

And then she laid her head back on the pillow and closed her eyes. Looking like she belonged there.

Derrick blew out a long, slow, steadying breath as he closed the bedroom door. He rested his forehead on the cool wood. The attraction he felt to Samona was indefinable, and it shook him to the core. Samona was intriguing, tempting—everything she shouldn't be, given the reason he was in this apartment. But that didn't seem to matter to his body.

Somehow, some way, he had to control his wayward feelings. He had to think like Derrick Lawson, the cop. Not Derrick Cunningham, the writer who found his neighbor a little too interesting.

"Stop pacing, will you? You're making me dizzy."

Alex's eyes narrowed as he looked at Marie. Sometimes, he didn't understand her. She knew how important it was to get his share of the jewelry. *Their* share. Yet all she wanted to do nowadays was nag him. "I'm thinking, all right?"

"For goodness' sake, you'd think we didn't find anything at Samona's place."

"What's your problem?" Marie was getting on his last nerve. Maybe life would be simpler if he just got rid of her. He had taken care of that Milano woman. He could do it again if he had to. "Forget Samona."

"Why should I? You can't."

"Not that again. I already told you she means nothing to me other than being my ticket to freedom."

Marie rose from the kitchen table and approached him. "Really? You don't find her attractive?"

Alex sneered. "Why are you doing this? Why are you acting so crazy?"

Marie exhaled harshly and placed a hand on his arm. "I just want all this over with. I want you back. Us. It seems to me you only care about Roger and Samona."

Alex drew her into his arms, rolling his eyes when she couldn't see. She was becoming a weak link and he was tired of pampering her. "Don't you get it? The way I see it, when we're through with her, she's gonna be going to jail for robbery and murder. Roger left us the perfect scapegoat. You told me that yourself. So, I'm damn well gonna use it. All I care about is getting what's owed to me, and then getting out of town. With you."

Marie sighed. "I know."

"Tell me you're ready to do this, Marie. This thing is almost over. I can feel it. But I need you. You can't go soft on me now."

"I know. I won't."

"Good. Because we have to do this tomorrow. The sooner we get what we want, the sooner we can start our life somewhere warm."

Marie looked at him, a weak smile playing on her lips. "You really think that her contact will be in that hotel room tomorrow?"

Alex nodded. He was certain of that fact. The one good thing that had come of today was what he and Marie had found on the notepad at Samona's apartment: a hotel name, a time, and the name "Evelyn Cooper." Tomorrow, he would pay a visit to this Evelyn character. He couldn't explain the feeling in his gut, but he was sure Evelyn was connected to Roger. Maybe Roger would be at the hotel, too. His jaw flinched at the thought of seeing him again. The louse would regret ripping him off.

"I'm sure of that," Alex said. "Tomorrow, we're gonna get what's ours."

CHAPTER FOURTEEN

Desperate. Whoever had ransacked Samona's apartment was desperate, Derrick thought as he rummaged through her place, trying to get it into a manageable state. Her things had been thrown aside in a panic, not carefully searched. That told him the person or persons who had been here hadn't known what they were looking for. Rather, they had been searching for some type of clue to further whatever their purpose was.

It was early and Samona was still sleeping. Sometime during the night he had decided to wake before dawn and begin the task of putting her apartment back together. He thought that would be a nice surprise for her. After how frightened she'd been yesterday, he couldn't see her trying to put this place back together on her own.

He had also decided not to tell Mrs. Jefferson about the incident because he didn't want to alarm her. She may just insist on calling the police, and Derrick respected Samona's desire not to involve them. At least not yet.

Not involving the police meant his cover would not be

blown. Not now, anyway. Deep down, he admitted to himself that he wasn't ready to end his relationship with Samona, whatever that relationship was.

He had been working on the place for more than two hours, and still it looked like a tornado hit it. Every time he stopped and thought about what had happened, his stomach tightened into a painful knot. Samona wasn't safe. He didn't know what the person responsible for this wanted, but it was clear Samona wasn't safe while this person knew where she lived.

Why he cared was something he didn't want to think about. People like Samona—criminals—deserved what they got. Yet Derrick's heart wouldn't reconcile that belief with his brain.

He took a break and stretched. He'd never been in a situation like this before; he'd never felt so confused. He was a cop and knew what he was supposed to do. But he had never in his life felt so ambiguous. Part of him wanted to arrest Samona as soon as possible. Part of him couldn't imagine putting her away for the rest of her life.

And then there was that darn attraction he felt for her. He couldn't understand it. Didn't want to. He wanted to forget it. But even as he thought of Samona, he pictured her in his bed, sleeping, leaving her honeyed scent on his pillows. He pictured her smiling at him. He remembered the way her lips felt under his, soft, yielding to his mouth. Kissing Samona had stirred powerful feelings within him.

Sexual feelings. That's all it was. Derrick felt a modicum of relief as that thought hit him. Samona was a beautiful woman and it was natural to feel some sort of attraction to her. After all, he hadn't been with a woman for a very long time. His work was demanding and he had no time to date. The only serious dating he had done had been during his college years, after which he'd joined the police force and dedicated himself to his job. In recent years there'd been the odd date here and there, but nothing serious. Most of those women he hadn't seen again. So why, especially considering the fact that Samona was under police investigation, could he not wait to see her again?

He was going to go crazy here, alone in Samona's apartment. Walking to the phone, he picked up the receiver and dialed the station. He asked for Nick Burns.

It took Nick more than a minute to answer, and he contemplated hanging up. Just as he was about to, he heard Nick's voice. "Burns," he said. "It's Lawson."

"Hey, Lawson. How's it going?"

"Not good, man. Not good."

"Uh oh. Ms. Gray?"

"Yeah. I have to tell you, Burns, the more time I spend with her the harder it is to believe that she was involved in this crime at all."

"Why not?"

"Because." Derrick searched for the right words to say. "Because she just doesn't seem the type. I don't know how she ever got involved with that Roger character, but being with her, talking with her . . . she really doesn't seem capable of anything so heinous."

"Lawson, you've got to remain objective. I know this woman is a looker, but you have to see past that. Think of Milano. Brutally murdered. She didn't deserve that."

"I have thought of Mrs. Milano. Every day. But I'm telling you, I really have my doubts."

"Oh God. You're falling for her."

"I didn't say that."

"You didn't have to. It's pretty obvious."

Derrick groaned. "Yes, I think she's attractive. Who wouldn't? But that's all. You know me better than that. I'm a trained cop. I know how to do my job."

"And you're also human. If for whatever reason you think you can't be objective, you better let Captain Boyle know. I'm telling you, man. You don't want to get burned."

"I won't." The thought of walking away from this case

now wasn't one Derrick wanted to consider. "She's starting to trust me."

Nick chuckled. "You don't want to leave her. You've got it bad, man."

"You're wrong. Trust me." The words sounded false even to Derrick's own ears.

"All right. I'll give you the benefit of the doubt. But I'll also give you a warning. Watch yourself. This is a big case and a lot is riding on you. You don't want to blow it."

"I hear you. Thanks for your concern."

"Who are you talking to?"

Spinning around, Derrick replaced the receiver. Samona stood about five feet behind him, her clothes wrinkled from sleeping in them. His heart raced. How much had she heard?

"Derrick? You didn't call the police, did you?"

"No." Not for the reason she had thought. "That was . . . a friend."

Samona nodded. "I see."

He wasn't sure if she believed him. "You don't mind that I used your phone, do you?"

"No." Placing her hands on her hips, Samona looked around the living room. "Why didn't you wake me?"

Derrick's heart rate returned to normal. Thank God, Samona had not overheard more of his conversation. He approached her. "I figured you needed your sleep. I'm sure this has been very stressful for you, so I just wanted to help out."

"You didn't have to do this."

"I know."

Samona opened her mouth to speak, closed it, then opened it again. "Why?"

"Why did I do this?"

"Why are you being so nice to me?"

Why indeed? It was a question on his mind as well. In two strides, he closed the distance between them and placed his hands on her shoulders. The skin beneath her tank top was soft and smooth beneath his fingers. He wanted to kiss her again, to feel her surrender to him once more. But the conversation with Nick was still on his mind. "I just want to help. Is that a good enough reason?"

There was a flash of disappointment in her eyes. His throat tightened. Maybe she was hoping for a different answer. Why did it matter to him if she was?

Samona said, "I guess so." She shrugged away from his touch. "Well, let's get to work. There's a lot more to do here."

A few hours later, Samona's apartment was looking a lot better. Except for helping to put her bed back together, Derrick had avoided her bedroom. She wondered why.

Derrick was so confusing. One minute, it seemed as though he liked her. The next minute, she wasn't sure if he was being anything other than a friendly neighbor.

But he kissed you, a voice in her head told her. *Twice.* She paused over her dresser, closing her eyes for a moment as she remembered his kisses. The first had been the kind that said you were interested; the second had been the kind that could cause two people to lose control. Derrick had stirred an overwhelming passion within her. Yesterday, she had wanted him so badly. Despite her better judgment, she very well may have made love to him if she hadn't found her apartment ransacked.

Samona wrapped her arms around her body. What was it about Derrick? Even when Mark had kissed her, she hadn't felt the all-consuming emotions she had felt when Derrick pulled her into his arms.

She wasn't supposed to feel anything for anyone. Not now. Not with the cloud of suspicion hanging over her head. She didn't have anything to offer a man like Derrick.

And it certainly wouldn't be fair to him to get involved with him when she knew any day she could be arrested.

The thought of getting arrested, the thought of losing Derrick, made her stomach swirl. For a moment in time she had let herself believe that maybe . . . maybe she would be able to love. Be loved. Have a normal life. Now, she realized what a fool she was.

She should go out to the living room and tell Derrick that she couldn't see him anymore. There was no point beginning something when she could see no future between them. That wasn't fair to either of them. But despite her thoughts, Samona stood rooted to the floor in her bedroom. How could she tell Derrick to leave when he was the best thing that had happened to her?

That thought scared her. Scared her because there was a very real chance that she could lose him. Lose him before she had a chance to love him.

Maybe that was for the best. But even though her brain said that, her heart couldn't accept it. When had her feelings for Derrick grown so strong?

When Samona heard the light rapping on her door, she jumped, throwing a hand to her chest.

"Sorry," Derrick said. "I didn't mean to startle you."

Facing him, she ran a hand over her hair. "That's okay."

He stayed at the door. "Is everything all right?"

"Yes. I was just thinking." *About you. Us.*

Derrick's gaze fell to the floor. Samona wondered what he was thinking. After several seconds, he finally looked at her. "The living room looks much better. And the kitchen. Your papers and artwork are in a pile on the coffee table, since I didn't know where you wanted them."

"Thanks."

"You're welcome. I was going to take off now, if you're okay."

"I'm fine. Go ahead."

"I can come back later."

"That's okay. I can handle the rest from here." *If you were talking about something else, please tell me now, Derrick.*

Derrick nodded. "All right. I'll see you later."

Samona saw him to the door. He didn't kiss her. He didn't even look at her with any special interest. She tried not to show her disappointment. She had no ties to Derrick Cunningham.

The instant he was gone, she hugged her elbows and leaned forward, hanging her head to her knees. That didn't relieve her stress much, but it helped her regain focus. She could not let Derrick have such a powerful effect on her.

Easier said than done. Groaning, she realized she needed to talk to someone. She rushed to the phone and called Jennifer. School was barely over and Jennifer might not be home yet, but Samona hoped she was. She could use her friend's advice.

When Jennifer answered the phone, Samona was relieved. "Jen, I'm so glad I reached you."

"Hey, Sammi. Everything okay?"

"I am so confused."

"Go ahead," Jennifer said. "I'm listening."

Samona walked across the room with the phone, then sank into the sofa, sighing. "Remember Derrick, my new neighbor?"

"How could I forget?"

"Well . . . Gosh, I can't believe I'm gonna say this." Samona paused briefly, then continued. "Despite everything, how messed up my life is right now, I think I'm falling for him."

"Falling for him as in you think he's cute? Or falling for him as in you're *falling* for him?"

"Falling for him as in . . . I can't stop thinking about him. Not at night. Not during the day. He's so attractive. But it's not only that. He's such a nice guy."

"Mmm hmm."

"Is that all you have to say?"

"Do you want me to say I'm surprised?"

Samona ran a hand through her hair. "I don't know. Yes. Yes, you should be surprised. I am."

"As you said, he's very attractive. And you are still a woman—one who's very much alive. You'd have to be blind to not notice that he's hot. Though I didn't get a chance to talk to him, just by looking at him I could tell he's one of the nice guys. So, no. I'm not surprised."

"This is scary. What I feel for Derrick I never felt for Mark."

"Ouch. So this is serious."

"I don't know. Maybe."

Jennifer asked, "How does he feel about you?"

"He's kissed me. Twice."

"Hmm. Lucky you."

"Stop it. You're happily involved."

"But I'm not dead." Samona could hear a smile in her friend's voice.

Samona frowned. "What do I do?"

"I say go with the flow."

"I want to. But how can I? My life is so screwed up. Any minute, the cops might find more evidence and arrest me. I couldn't take that—seeing the disappointment in Derrick's eyes if that happened."

"If the police had anything on you, they would have arrested you by now. You know it, and I know it."

Samona thought the same thing, but didn't truly feel free yet. Wouldn't until she was officially cleared. "I don't want to count my eggs before they're hatched. I can't help thinking that this is too good to be true. That it's all going to blow up in my face."

"Then why don't you tell him?"

"Are you crazy? I can't."

"Why not? You know what I say about honesty. Everything's possible if there's honesty in a relationship. And you're not guilty, so you have nothing to fear.''

"It's not that simple.''

"I know it's hard. But I've always believed in taking chances. Go for it. Don't let Roger ruin your life any more than he already has.''

"You're right. I know you are. But I'm afraid.''

"Afraid of what? Afraid that you might find the happiness you want? Or afraid that Derrick doesn't really feel for you the way you feel for him?''

Samona paused. After a long moment she said quietly, "Afraid of making another mistake. Of being a fool. Again.''

"What does your gut say?''

"I don't know. I only know that I really like him. But after what happened with Roger . . .''

"With Roger, you were never sure. Remember? You told me you were seeing him but you felt something wasn't right? Is that how you feel about Derrick?''

Samona didn't hesitate. "Not at all.''

"Then, my dear friend, I think you have your answer.''

Evelyn sat on the edge of the hotel's bed, her hands folded in her lap, thinking. If she could turn back the clock, she would not have hurt her sister. She had been wrong to go after her boyfriend, and knew Samona had been devastated when Evelyn married Mark. She had thought that seeing pain in Samona's eyes would make her happy, take away the bitterness she felt toward her, but it didn't. It only hurt her.

It wasn't that Evelyn didn't love Mark. She did, truly. But she should have made sure he ended his relationship with her sister before she ever dated him. So much pain could have been avoided.

Evelyn leaned forward. She wondered if God was punishing her for hurting her sister. Now, the one thing she wanted more than anything in the world she couldn't have: She and Mark couldn't have children.

There was a knock at the door. Her heart fluttering, she closed her eyes. She had been anxiously awaiting this moment since Samona had called from the hotel lobby. Finally, she would see her sister again after two long years. After Samona had left their parents' funeral without so much as a good-bye.

What would she look like? Thinner? Plumper? Visibly older? Maybe she had lost weight because of everything she was going through with the criminal investigation. While Evelyn ate when nervous or stressed, Samona didn't.

Would Samona smile when she saw her, or scowl? Or would she simply be indifferent? Evelyn's stomach lurched. She could handle intense emotions—anything but indifference.

Rising from the bed, Evelyn smoothed her elegant slacks and walked slowly to the door. Her nerves were tattered and even her hands shook. God, she was nervous. This was an important visit—a turning point in their relationship. She hoped that Samona would want to work things out, that she wasn't here to tell her she never wanted to see her again.

There was another knock. Evelyn took a brief moment to check out her appearance in the bathroom mirror. She looked fine. *Just answer the door. Nothing is worse than not knowing.* She and her sister had a lot of issues to deal with, but they were the only blood family they had. It was time they made amends.

Evelyn steadied her hand and turned the knob, her heart racing. Before she could fully open the door, it was shoved open violently, throwing her backward. As she scrambled to regain her balance, a man and a woman marched into her room. A man and a woman she did not know.

Something was terribly wrong. She glanced at the intruders for only a moment longer before bolting for the door. She didn't make it. The man grabbed her forcefully, whirling her around. He punched her in the face, then threw her to the floor.

The room started to spin.

"Don't even think of doing that again, and don't even think of screaming. I have a gun, and I'm not afraid to use it."

Stunned, Evelyn merely stared at him. Who was this jerk? Who was this woman searching her hotel room? She was more angry than afraid, but she was no fool.

"Where's the jewelry?"

Blood from her nose trickled into her mouth. Her chest heaved. She didn't respond.

The man stooped beside her and grabbed her face. He squeezed it harshly, digging his dirty nails into her skin. "I said, where's the jewelry?"

"I don't know what you're talking about." Blood spilled from her mouth as she spoke. Oh God, there was so much blood.

"Wrong answer." He backhanded her across the face.

Angry tears filled Evelyn's eyes.

The woman spoke then. "We know you know where it is. And if you value your life, you'll tell us."

Evelyn's mind raced to find an answer that would satisfy them. Suddenly, she knew her life depended on it. She could think of none. "I don't know."

"Where's Roger?"

"R–Roger? Roger who?"

The woman poked her head under the bed, then rose. "He's not here."

"Too chicken to face me, huh?" the man said to Evelyn.

"I don't know any Roger." But she did. The one Samona had been dating.

"Give Roger a message for me. Or his girlfriend Samona—whoever you're here to meet." Pure evil flashed in the man's eyes as he raised his hand, this time with his gun.

Evelyn's heart went berserk with fear. "God no!"

He struck her with the butt of the gun. Once, twice. Many more times. She tried to use her arms to block the blows, but he was still able to make contact with her head and her face. Her blood spattered everywhere.

At some point, her body became numb and she stopped feeling. Slowly stopped acknowledging what was happening. Then finally, a welcoming, painless darkness overcame her.

CHAPTER FIFTEEN

Samona sat on her bed with her arms wrapped around her knees, wishing she could pinpoint the moment Derrick had crawled under her skin and made his way to her heart. She couldn't. It didn't matter. He was there now.

In her heart. She blew out a shaky breath. So much was wrong in her life and she was so afraid. Afraid to love. Afraid she'd never love again. Afraid she'd lose the one good thing in her life before she ever really had it.

Derrick . . . She didn't know what it was about him, but it was something. Maybe his charming smile. Maybe his compelling eyes. Maybe his cute dimples. Maybe . . .

The phone rang, jarring her from her musings. Glancing at the wall clock, she saw that it was after six in the evening. Where had the time gone, she wondered as she grabbed the receiver. "Hello?"

"Hello, Samona. I'm glad I caught you home."

Immediately, Samona's throat tightened and she couldn't draw breath. Blood pounded in her ears. Her hands shook and she barely held on to the receiver.

"Samona, it's Mark."

Somehow she was able to swallow, wet her throat. "Y–yes," she croaked. "I–I know."

Mark. The one man she had loved. The man who hadn't had the courtesy to officially dump her before he'd started seeing her sister. Mark, the man she'd hoped to marry, but who had married her sister. Mark, whom she hadn't seen nor spoken to since her parents' funeral. Why now was he calling her?

"Samona, I'm calling about Evelyn."

Of course. Evelyn. The sister he had married. He probably wanted to reach her in Chicago. Maybe she wasn't in her hotel room and Mark thought she was with her.

She didn't care. She didn't know why her body was acting like she did. She was over Mark. But, God help her, the betrayal still hurt.

"Samona, are you there?"

"Hmm . . . yes. Yes, I'm here."

"Did you hear what I said?"

The urgency in his voice caused a shiver of dread to wash over her. "What is it? What's wrong?"

"Your sister's in the hospital."

"What?!"

"I got a call from the police about an hour ago. Evelyn's been beaten up pretty bad."

"Oh my God." She felt dizzy, winded. "Beat up? Where? Why?"

"I don't know the details. I only know she's at Cook County Hospital."

"Oh God. Okay. Let me grab a pen." She put down the phone and searched for a pen and paper. With everything in disarray, she couldn't find one. Her hands were shaking so badly.

She stopped. Inhaled. Exhaled. Concentrated. In the living room on her coffee table, she found a pen and paper. She hurried back to the phone in her bedroom.

Mark gave her Evelyn's room number. He also told her that he was at the airport and his flight would be arriving in a few hours. "I'll meet you at the hospital," he said. "I'm on my way now."

Samona hung up and searched for her purse. It wasn't in her bedroom. Frustrated, she squeezed her forehead and looked around. Where was it?

The living room. She hurried there and found her purse on the sofa. Exactly where she'd left it.

She felt lost, terrified. Almost as disoriented as she'd felt the day Roger had put a gun to her head. Her sister was seriously injured. It was hard to believe.

What if she had died in the attack?

Samona shook her head, dismissing the thought. Her sister wasn't dead. She was at the hospital and she had to get to her. Now. Her hands still shaking, Samona dug her car keys out of her purse.

Somehow she managed to lock her door. She turned to run down the stairs and stopped. Instead, she headed up the stairs to Derrick's door.

Her fingers were so jittery they were almost numb. She could barely feel them when they knocked.

It seemed like hours before Derrick opened the door. His eyes bulged when he saw her. "Samona. What is it?"

"My sister." Her voice sounded hollow to her ears. "She's hurt. Bad."

"Where is she?"

"The hospital."

"Which one?"

"C—Cook County."

Saying the words again didn't make it real. It seemed like she was caught in a bizarre dream that wouldn't end.

"Gimme a second. I'll drive you." Derrick disappeared into the apartment and returned moments later, his keys in hand. Placing a hand on her back, he gently guided her down the stairs.

Samona was barely aware of anything during the drive to the hospital. She was numb, afraid to feel. But when they entered the hospital room and she saw her sister on the bed, her face cut and badly bruised, sadness overwhelmed her. And guilt. A painful lump lodged in her throat.

After all this time, she hadn't known what she'd feel when she saw her sister again. She certainly hadn't expected to feel as much as she did. For years she had told herself that she didn't care about Evelyn. That she didn't need her in her life. But seeing her sister horribly beaten proved two things to her. She loved her and missed her. She was the only family she had left. Today she had almost lost her without ever making things right.

She felt Derrick's hands on her shoulders. Felt him squeeze gently in a silent show of support. She leaned into him for strength, then moved to the side of the bed where her sister lay.

An oxygen mask covered Evelyn's nose and mouth. Her closed eyes were severely bruised and swollen. So were her lips, from what Samona could see beneath the mask.

Good God, who had done this to her sister? Though she had wanted to remain strong, tears spilled onto her cheeks. Tears for Evelyn and for herself.

Samona held a hand over Evelyn's body, afraid to touch her. Finally, she brought her hand to her sister's forehead, brushing her hair off her face. Evelyn didn't respond. She was still. Seemingly lifeless.

Samona thought of her parents. Wondered how bad they had looked after the accident. She hadn't been allowed to see them and the caskets had been closed. All she could do was hug their coffins and say her final good-byes. She had felt so helpless. She felt helpless now.

Derrick ran a hand down Samona's arm, but she didn't turn. In slow, rhythmic movements, she stroked her sister's forehead.

"Samona, I'm going to find your sister's doctor."

She nodded absently.

As Derrick left the room, his own stomach coiled. Samona was in pain. Nobody should have to suffer the way she was. She had lost her parents, and now her sister was critically injured.

He remembered all too well the day his own father had died. At first, all he could feel was disbelief. Then, he had comforted his mother because she'd been devastated. It was only after his father had been buried that the reality of the situation had finally hit him. Alone in his room, he had cried. His father had died of a heart attack at the age of forty-seven. He'd had symptoms but ignored them, dismissing them as insignificant, and ultimately paid with his life.

That was twelve years ago, when Derrick was a teenager. After his father's sudden death, he had vowed to live a healthier life. Eat well and exercise. Get regular checkups.

"Hello, Detective Lawson."

Derrick spun around and faced the petite Chinese nurse he had seen on several occasions when he'd come to this hospital's emergency room. Immediately, he looked around, worried that Samona might be in earshot. She wasn't.

He looked at her name tag. "Pearl. Hello."

"Are you here on an investigation today?"

"Actually," Derrick began, "I'm here with a friend. Her sister was badly beaten. I was just about to look for her doctor."

"Who's the patient?"

"All I know is that her name is Evelyn."

"That must be Evelyn Cooper. She was attacked in her hotel room. Somehow she managed to make it to the phone before she lost consciousness."

Derrick's brow furrowed. Her hotel room. That struck him as an odd place to get attacked. Either she was at some sleazy motel, or she knew her attacker. "Do you know which hotel?"

Pearl shook her head. "I can't remember the name. But it's one of the posh ones downtown." She shook her head ruefully, then said, "Let me see if I can find her doctor for you."

Evelyn's doctor was a black man in his fifties. He shook Derrick's hand and said, "I'm Dr. Walker. Are you a family member of Mrs. Cooper's?"

"I'm Detective Lawson with the Chicago Police Department." Derrick produced his badge for verification.

"A police officer was here earlier regarding Mrs. Cooper and I spoke with her."

"I'm not here in an official capacity. I'm here with the victim's sister, Samona Gray."

"I see."

"Naturally, Samona is very distraught and is by her sister's side. I was hoping you could tell me the extent of Evelyn's injuries."

"Certainly, Detective. Let me first say that Mrs. Cooper is a very lucky woman. The beating she received was a vicious one and could have had much more serious consequences. She's in critical but stable condition. She has a concussion and hasn't yet regained consciousness but I expect she will soon. Unfortunately, she also suffered extensive injuries to her left cornea. I don't want to alarm you, but it is possible that she may lose an eye. I won't know that for sure until we run a few more tests."

Derrick planted his hands on his hips as he contemplated the doctor's words. "That's pretty bad."

"Yes, it is. But as I said, I won't know the extent of the injury until the results of further tests. I'm hopeful. Evelyn is a fighter. Quite miraculously, she was able to call the hotel's front desk before she passed out. They then called the ambulance."

Judging by Samona's reaction, Derrick knew this new

development would be especially hard for her to deal with. Wondering what to do, he bit his bottom lip. He didn't want to give her bad news, but he wouldn't lie to her. Not about this. Maybe he would wait until absolutely necessary before letting her know the extent of her sister's injuries.

"Any suspects?" he asked.

"None that I know of."

"Thanks, Dr. Walker." Derrick left the man and went to a pay phone. He called the district that would have dealt with this incident and spoke with Amanda Healy, the investigating officer. She told him that so far there were no suspects, but the crime unit was at the hotel testing for prints and looking for evidence.

Derrick hung up and folded his arms over his chest. He had goose bumps on the back of his neck. He didn't like this. Evelyn Cooper was in town on a business trip and had been assaulted? What were the chances of that?

Derrick's gut was telling him this was more than a random assault. His gut told him that somehow this had something to do with Samona. Something to do with the Milano case.

In the almost three hours that Samona had been by her sister's side, Evelyn had not regained consciousness. Samona had tried talking to her like she saw people do in the movies, but Evelyn had not responded.

Samona threw a quick glance at Derrick, who stood beside her. More than once she had told him that she would be okay, that he could leave, but he had refused. A smile touched her lips as she remembered. Truth be told, she didn't know how she would have gotten through the day if it weren't for Derrick. Thanks to him, she didn't feel as scared as she had initially. He had been gentle when he'd told her that her sister might lose an eye and had convinced her not to worry about that fact until necessary.

Though she'd been in pain, Derrick had made her realize that the most important thing was that Evelyn would be okay. Still, Samona wouldn't feel truly relieved until her sister woke up.

The sound of voices drew her attention to the door. Seconds later, the curtained partition opened and a nurse entered with Mark. Immediately, Samona ran to him, throwing her arms around his neck. "Mark. . . ."

He kissed her cheek and squeezed her tightly for a long moment. "How is she? Really?"

She hadn't seen him in two years, hadn't wanted to because of his betrayal, but surprisingly Samona felt no bitterness. Once, his kiss and his embrace would have ignited some feeling within her. Now, she felt nothing. Nothing but a sense of happiness that the man who loved her sister was here for Evelyn. Pulling back, she attempted a smile. "Evelyn's going to be okay, Mark."

Derrick approached Mark and said, "I'm Derrick. Samona's friend."

"Mark." He shook Derrick's hand. "Mark Cooper. Thanks for being here. I appreciate it. Samona, the doctor wasn't available when I arrived. Did he tell you anything about Evelyn's condition?"

She told him everything, watched as pain contorted his features as he learned the extent of Evelyn's injuries. Samona wished she could do more for him, but she couldn't.

When she finished her story, Mark nodded tightly, his eyes glazed as though he couldn't believe what he'd heard. He ran a hand over his short hair and blew out a ragged breath, then started for his wife's bed. Leaning forward, he kissed Evelyn's forehead, whispering something Samona couldn't hear. Then he lifted his wife's hand into his.

Samona jumped when Derrick ran his hands down her arms. The next moment she leaned into him for support. This was a weird moment when past and present merged.

She felt a strange sense of bittersweet happiness watching Mark with Evelyn. Surprisingly, her heart felt light, free of the burden that had weighed her down for years. It was like she had gone through an instant metamorphosis. The bitterness and anger she had once felt toward Mark and Evelyn seemed to float from her body and dissolve in the air.

Mark was her past. He was her sister's husband. He loved Evelyn, and Samona could accept that now.

Derrick was her present. As she brought a hand on to his where it rested on her arm, Samona couldn't help thinking that the reason for this metamorphosis involved Derrick. Involved her feelings for him.

She couldn't deny now that she was falling in love with him. Silently, she wondered, *Will Derrick be my future?*

It was almost an hour since two orderlies and a nurse came to take Evelyn for testing. Mark walked back and forth, pacing the floor. Samona sat on a chair watching him. Derrick stood, watching her.

Samona didn't have to tell him that she had once been in love with Mark. It was obvious. Had been from the moment she had run into his arms and thrown her arms around him.

Derrick knew it didn't make sense, but he'd felt a twinge of jealousy when the two had embraced. It wasn't that he really felt threatened; Mark was married to Evelyn. But he wondered how close Samona and Mark had been. Had he been her one true love?

Derrick rubbed his tired eyes. He sensed Mark and Samona had been very close. If Mark had dumped her and married her sister, that was probably the reason why Samona and Evelyn were not close. And for Samona to be angry with her sister years afterward meant that she'd had strong feelings for Mark. No doubt, she had loved him. He didn't know for sure, and at this point he could only guess, but Derrick figured Mark had probably been Samona's one true love. Derrick had heard stories about how hard it was to get over one's true love—he knew it first-hand. But he had gotten over Whitney. Had Samona gotten over Mark?

His thoughts were interrupted when Evelyn was wheeled back into the room. She looked the same as when she had left: not unconscious.

Derrick, Samona and Mark all faced the nurse. She explained that the results of the tests would not be known for a couple of hours.

Mark sighed, exasperated, then immediately went to his wife's side. Samona walked to Derrick and he took her in his arms.

Facing them, Mark said, "You two don't have to stay here. Go on home. I'll call you if there's any change."

"No." Samona shook her head. "I want to be here."

Mark held Samona's gaze for a long moment, flashed her a weak smile, then turned back to Evelyn.

Derrick wondered about the look. Wondered why he cared.

Samona didn't know how much longer she would last. She was fading, despite her desire to stay awake until there was a change in her sister's condition. It would be so easy to fall asleep now, with Derrick's arms around her as she sat on his lap.

The intimacy between them wasn't forced. In fact, Mark must think they were an old couple. If Mark was thinking about anything other than Evelyn.

Derrick yawned and Samona knew he, too, was still awake. She snuggled against him, wondering when she had become so comfortable with him. Wondering why just being near him made her feel better.

Mark stood and stretched. Then he walked toward her

and Derrick. His eyes were red; he was tired too. This was a long night and it wasn't over yet.

"Why don't you go home?" Mark suggested. "There's nothing you can do now. Get some sleep and come back tomorrow."

Derrick shifted beneath her, then placed his hands on her shoulders. "What do you say, Samona? Mark is right. You need to get some sleep."

Samona closed her eyes and thought long and hard. There was always tomorrow, but what if Evelyn took a turn for the worse during the night? She didn't know what to do.

All at once, a picture of her parents entered her mind and a feeling of peace washed over her. Somehow she knew then that Evelyn would be okay. She could feel her parents' spirits in the room with her as though they were actually there. They were watching over Evelyn, protecting her.

"Okay," she said. "Let's go."

She hugged Mark, then went to her sister and kissed her cheek. After promising to return as soon as she could tomorrow, she and Derrick left.

At some point during the drive home, Derrick reached out and took her hand. Samona looked at him, thinking he might say something, but he only smiled softly. The rest of the way home he held her hand, silently offering her comfort as he had for the past several hours.

Samona's heart felt full. Derrick hadn't spoken the words, but she felt loved. More loved than she had ever felt with Mark. Derrick had been there for her during the entire day without any complaints. Not only had he offered her support, he'd offered her hope. With him, her world didn't seem as dark as it once had been.

As they climbed the steps in their Oak Park home, Derrick said, "My bed is yours tonight—if you want it."

Samona's body thrummed with longing at his words.

For an instant, she let herself fantasize. She let herself believe that Derrick was inviting her to share his bed—with him. God, how she wanted to wrap her arms around him and lose herself in this man.

"I don't mind taking the couch," he added.

The fantasy died. Samona sighed. She couldn't stay in Derrick's apartment and not be with him. After the trying day with her sister, she would want his comforting arms around her. "Thanks, but I'll stay at my place tonight. I'll be okay."

"You're sure?"

Samona nodded.

"Okay. I'll see you tomorrow."

He kissed her forehead, a chaste kiss, but one that set off sparks in her body. "Yes, tomorrow."

She watched him walk off until she couldn't see him anymore. But she didn't enter her apartment then. She stayed in the hallway, her back propped against the wall, listening. She heard him open his door above her.

When his door clicked shut and she heard the lock turn, Samona released the breath she didn't know she was holding, and closed her eyes. As she stood in the hallway, her eyes closed, her heart beating a musical waltz in her heart, Samona knew at that moment that she was in love.

CHAPTER SIXTEEN

Someone was in her room, watching her. Someone with hard, cold eyes. Oh God . . .

Anxiety seizing her, Samona's eyes flew open but she didn't dare move. She could see nothing in the dark room, hear nothing but the windows rattling in protest as the night wind howled. Yet something had awakened her. An eerie feeling overcame her and her heart raced. Was her sister okay?

She sat up and was about to reach for the phone but stopped. Were those footsteps she heard? Fear skittered down her spine and she held her breath.

When in the dark night she heard nothing else, Samona let out a relieved breath. She was being ridiculous. Who would be in her apartment?

The person who had turned her place upside down.

She shook her head. No, she couldn't believe that. She was safe. She had to be. She was worried about her sister. That was all.

As she sat in the dark room trying to detect any foreign

sound, a horrible thought invaded her mind. It caused goose bumps to pop out all over her skin. Her sister had been attacked *after* her apartment had been ransacked. She'd had a note by the phone with the information about where Evelyn was staying. Samona's chest heaved as a shiver of nervous dread passed over her. God no. It was too horrible to be true.

But she hadn't seen the note. Not that she could have found it in the mess, but still she worried. Was it possible that the person who had broken into her apartment had attacked her sister?

It makes sense.

Right now, she wished she had stayed with Derrick tonight. She was afraid—too afraid to even leave her bed. She would be afraid until she awoke in the morning and found she was still alive.

Maybe she was overreacting. Maybe the events of recent days had her more frightened than she cared to admit. Nobody had been in her room. Her sister's attack had nothing to do with her.

Samona clung to that thought, but that didn't make her feel any better. Her gut told her something was wrong.

She was cold. There must be a draft from the window. Lying back, Samona pulled the blanket up to her neck, wrapping it around her shoulders to shield off the chill. But as she did, she couldn't be sure if the cold was really from the wind, or from somewhere deep within her.

"Where are you going?" the man asked.

"I'm leaving!" the woman shouted as she grabbed her clothes from the floor. Her neck hurt from where he had grabbed her. She wasn't going to stick around to let him treat her like he owned her. "You're crazy. I didn't know how much—"

"You're not going anywhere."

She screamed as he seized her arm harshly. "Let me go. I don't want to see you anymore. Okay? That's all. I just want out. . . ."

He wrapped a thick hand around her thin neck. "Why are you doing this? You know I love you."

"You only love you. Not me, not anybody else. And I'm tired of it. I'm tired of your need to control."

"Really?"

He squeezed her neck and she almost gagged. She didn't like what she saw in his eyes. Hatred. Evil. She was talking to a dangerous man, she realized. She needed to take a different approach. "Look, I just need some time."

"You said you were leaving me."

"I . . . I didn't mean that. I just meant . . ."

He squeezed harder. "You wouldn't be just saying that now?"

"No," she wailed. She grabbed at his hands. "St–stop. Y–you're hurt–ing me."

He slapped her then. Her hand flew to her cheek and she looked at him, the man she had loved. Who was he? She didn't know him anymore.

Slowly, she began to back away from him. He walked toward her with confidence. Menacingly. Fear gripping her, she turned and ran.

He caught her in a few seconds. She screamed and scratched and kicked as he slapped and choked her. A kick landed in his groin and he yelled in pain.

She scrambled for the phone. Dialed 911.

"Derrick! Derrick, open up!"

When Derrick heard the pounding at the door, he threw off the covers and ran to open it. Samona rushed into his apartment, her eyes wide with fear. "Samona, what happened? Is it Evelyn?"

"No." Her chest rose and fell quickly with each rapid breath she inhaled.

"All right. Take a deep breath, then tell me what's going on."

"My apartment . . . someone was there last night. Someone . . ."

"Wait a minute. What do you mean? Someone was there while you were there? Or before you got there?"

Samona sobbed softly. "Last night, something awoke me. I thought . . . maybe someone had been there. But then I thought I was just overreacting. Then, when I woke up this morning, I found a note. . . ."

"Where?"

"On my kitchen counter."

Derrick placed his hands on Samona's trembling shoulders. "Samona, where is the note now?"

"Downstairs. With the dead rose."

"Dead rose?"

She sniffled and nodded.

"Can you show me?"

She drew in a deep breath. "Okay."

He took her hand and they walked down the stairs to her apartment door. It was open. Samona hadn't even stopped to close it on her way out.

The note and rose were on the kitchen counter as she said. Not only was the rose black and dried, its petals lay scattered. Leaning over the counter, but careful not to touch the surface, Derrick read the note.

What happened today was just a warning.
Next time we won't be so nice.
Give us what we want and everything will be okay. If you don't, you'll be sorry. We are very serious. We'll be in touch.

Smart, Derrick thought. Whoever had written the note had not implicated himself in any crime. Everything had been vague, with only enough information for the recipient to understand. But Derrick understood.

He said, "Did you touch anything?"

"No . . . I was too scared."

"Good. That was very good, Samona. You haven't tampered with the scene and now the police can dust for prints."

Samona's eyes flew to his. Confusion flashed in their depths. For a moment, Derrick's heart stopped. She knew. Knew he was a cop and that he had been lying to her.

But she said, "I . . . I can't."

Derrick's heart began beating, but he didn't know why he was relieved. Samona needed to contact the police. Needed to report this. With the attack on her sister, and now this rose and note, Derrick was certain that Samona's life was in danger. That she would find out he was a cop was a consequence he had to deal with. Right now, he only cared about her safety.

"Come here." He took her hand and led her to the living room. "We need to talk."

Samona looked at him, shaking her head. "Not here."

"Fine. Then we'll go to my apartment."

Samona agreed and they went upstairs. She sat on his sofa and he sat next to her. She linked her fingers together then rested her chin atop her hands. Derrick wondered how much more stress she could take before she completely broke down.

"Samona," he said. "Remember when I told you that I was here for you, that I would listen to you? I don't want to pressure you, but I think you should start talking. If not to me, then to the police. Whatever is going on here is very serious. I can't help but feel that you're in danger."

"I think so too."

"What does that note mean? What do you have that someone wants?"

Samona buried her face in her hands and moaned. Her head pounded and it felt like her last nerve was going to break. Why was all of this happening to her? She was a good person and she didn't deserve this. Finally, she said, "There's a lot you don't know about me, Derrick." She paused, afraid to go on. She couldn't take it if he turned her away now, even though she wouldn't blame him if he did. "You might not like this."

His body felt like a live wire, with energy flowing through him at rapid speed. This was the moment he had waited for. The moment she told him what he had been given the responsibility of finding out. Part of him wanted to stop her—he didn't want to know the truth now. Not if it could jeopardize what he was feeling for her. But he was a cop with a job to do. That came first. He would see this through to the end. He said softly, "Go on."

"The reason I can't call police is because they won't believe me."

"Why would you say that?" Derrick asked, although he knew the answer.

"Because . . ." Samona sighed. "Because they believe I'm responsible for a crime that took place just over two months ago. If I call them now, they won't help me. They'll probably throw me in jail."

Derrick tried to act as though this information came as a surprise. "What did you do?"

"Nothing!"

Samona brushed her hair back with both hands and for the first time Derrick saw the scar. It must have been from the robbery, where she had been injured. He said, "I'm sorry. I didn't mean to say that. I meant to ask what the police think you've done."

"Please, Derrick. Please tell me that you'll listen to what I'm about to say with an open mind."

"I will." Derrick meant it. Part of his heart hoped now that Samona would offer him the explanation he needed, a reason to believe in her innocence.

"Okay." She looked down at her fingers, then back at him. "The police think I was involved in a robbery and murder."

"Murder?" Derrick hoped he sounded shocked enough.

Samona's face contorted with grief. "Yes. Murder." Her voice cracked and she took a moment before she continued. "It's not true. I didn't do it. I could never . . ."

"What happened?"

She couldn't tell by looking in his eyes if he believed her. God, she hoped he did. She couldn't take it if he didn't. Not after he made her fall in love with him.

"I was dating this guy. It wasn't serious—I didn't want it to be. On April Fool's Day, he took me to a jewelry store." She laughed mirthlessly. "At first I actually thought he was thinking of buying me an engagement ring. I was worried that he was going to do that because I wasn't interested in him in that way. Little did I know he had other plans in mind."

"He wanted to rob the place."

"Yes. And because I was with him, the police think I was involved."

"Surely the police must understand you had nothing to do with it—that you were just a victim, right?"

"I tried to tell them that, but they didn't believe me. You see, a woman was murdered. The store's clerk. Roger—my ex-boyfriend—fled the scene and got away. The people in this city want to see someone pay for the crime. Because Roger is no longer here, that someone is me."

"I can't believe that."

"That's because you're from Toronto. You don't know what it was like here two months ago. Every paper had a picture of me on the front page. And when the police couldn't come up with any concrete evidence to arrest me, people were angry. I lost my job, my life . . ."

"You still have your life, Samona. And from what you tell me, it doesn't sound like the police have anything on you." Man, did he ever feel like the biggest heel. Here he was offering her comforting words when he was her enemy. Why did she have to trust him? It would be so much easier if she had been snarky with him, rude, unapproachable. Not sweet, loving, vulnerable.

"They were watching me for several weeks. I think that they're trying to find out where the jewelry is. If they can positively link me to the jewelry, then they can arrest me with enough proof to make everybody happy."

"What about the murder?"

"Well, the police can't find a murder weapon, so they can't prove I fired the gun that killed the store owner. What I didn't tell you is that my loving ex-boyfriend knocked me unconscious at the scene. I guess I'm lucky. If I hadn't been out cold, he probably would have killed me too."

"Are you saying you didn't see the murder?"

"I don't know who killed that woman. When that happened I was dead to the world. Thankfully. I don't think I could live with that memory. It was bad enough waking up and seeing the body when the police had arrived."

Samona realized then that Derrick wasn't looking at her with contempt. Her heart leaped with joy. He didn't hate her. That meant he must believe her.

"Wow," Derrick said. "And you know nothing about where this Roger character is now?"

"He's dead. Apparently he got killed while trying to escape the country on a boat. He's the one I was talking about the other day. . . ."

"What I don't get—and what the police probably don't get—is why this guy would have brought you along for a robbery if you weren't involved. I'm no criminal, but that doesn't make sense to me."

"I don't know. God, if I had known I never would have been there that day. But now that I think about it, I'm sure I was part of his sick plan all along. He probably planned to bring me along, knock me out and leave me there to take the blame."

"Sounds like a sick guy. How'd you get involved with him?"

"I had no clue that Roger was a criminal. Or anything other than a decent guy. He was just the uncle of one of the kids at my school—"

"School?" To a stranger, it would seem Derrick really did know nothing about Samona Gray. He was even surprising himself with how convincing he sounded.

Samona's eyes closed pensively then slowly reopened. "I'm a teacher. A teacher without a job because of all this. If I'm not officially cleared of this crime, I may never teach again."

She had answered all his questions without hesitation. Derrick wondered why the investigating officers hadn't believed her. She sounded convincing, seemed sincere.

"Do you believe me?"

Derrick paused. Thought hard. Tried to find a balance between what his cop head said and what his mind said now. He told her what she wanted to hear. "Yes. I believe you."

Samona sighed, relieved. "Thank you. You don't know how much that means to me."

"I think I do."

Her hand touched his face. Stroked softly. Derrick sucked in a breath as the soft scent of her skin drifted into his nose. Samona excited him. Overwhelmed him. One touch and he was lost.

"I don't know what it is about you." Her lips trembled and her eyes filled with tears. "I . . ."

He froze. "What?"

"I . . . I'm so glad I met you."

He should be happy. She was saving him from making the biggest mistake in his career. Instead he felt a mixture of emotions—anticipation, confusion, arousal, sadness.

He planted a soft kiss on her lips, a kiss that easily could have lasted longer but he didn't allow himself that pleasure. "How about we go see your sister?"

Nodding, Samona smiled. "Yes. Give me a minute to get into something decent and I'll be right back."

As she hurried off, Derrick lay his head back on the sofa and grimaced. He wished he had the guts to be as honest with her as she seemed to be with him. Wished he could follow his heart and tell her the truth about who he was. Maybe she wouldn't hate him if he told her now.

He thought of Captain Boyle, of the commander, of the mayor. These people expected a lot from him. Maybe too much.

He couldn't tell Samona. At least not yet.

CHAPTER SEVENTEEN

Samona sat by her sister's side while Mark slept in the armchair. When she and Derrick had arrived at the hospital, they had learned the good news. Not only had Evelyn regained consciousness, she wasn't going to lose her eye.

Mark had hugged her and said, "You were right. You said everything was going to be all right, and it is."

Samona had turned to Derrick and looked into his eyes. "Derrick was the one who convinced me not to worry," she'd told Mark. "He gave me strength."

Mark had smiled at Derrick. "Sounds like you're a special person."

Derrick had shrugged, and Samona had watched both him and Mark carefully. Though she didn't need his blessing, it was like Mark was telling her he approved of Derrick. If Mark had said those words even a month ago, she would have been tempted to give him a piece of her mind. Now, the irony of the situation made her smirk.

Mark ... Evelyn. Samona looked down at her sister. Evelyn lay sleeping peacefully, and she didn't look much different from last night. But she had awoken. And, according to Mark, when she woke up around four in the morning, she hadn't stopped talking. Now, Samona hoped she would awake with her at her side. She had a lot she wanted to say.

If Evelyn would let her. Her lips twisting in a wry grin, Samona acknowledged that that was one thing that was going to change. From now on, Samona wasn't going to be afraid to tell her sister how she felt. If her true feelings about any given situation were out in the open, then they could try to work out their problems. She'd always been a bit intimated by Evelyn, her older sister who seemed to do no wrong. Samona had found it hard to talk to Evelyn growing up. Then, after Evelyn had betrayed her with Mark, Samona had shut down her emotions where her sister was concerned. They had hardly spoken because Samona hadn't been able to see past the betrayal and hadn't wanted to find the true source of their problems. She hadn't been the only one—Evelyn had let their relationship deteriorate. Until now.

So, they had a lot of things to talk about. A lot of catching up to do as sisters. And Samona wanted to ask Evelyn about the attack. But most importantly, she wanted to tell her that she was going to be there for her from now on. Their problems were not too monumental to overcome.

Samona looked at her sister for a long moment. It wasn't going to be easy, she acknowledged. She couldn't expect to have a wonderful friendship with her sister overnight. But she had taken the first step in salvaging the relationship with her sister—forgiveness. The past was the past and it couldn't be changed but the future could and would be different.

Samona felt Derrick approach her even though she couldn't hear him. He said, "I'm going to the cafeteria to get some drinks. What would you like?"

"An orange juice, please."

He kissed the top of her head and heat flooded her. The way he would kiss her without notice, gently stroke her face, rub her arms—it was like he was her lover. He knew just what to do to make her feel better and when, as though he had been making her feel better for years.

"I'll be back as soon as I can."

Samona watched Derrick leave the room, hoping. Hoping she could have a future with him.

Evelyn stirred, and Samona's gaze immediately fell on her. Her heart beat rapidly with anticipation. After two years, she would finally speak to her sister face-to-face.

Evelyn shifted in the bed, made a face as though she was in pain, then settled. Samona wondered if she were actually going to wake up.

The next moment, Evelyn's eyelids snapped open. Looking around for a moment, it seemed she was trying to figure out where she was. Then her eyes rested on Samona.

She said softly, "Samona?"

"Yes, Evelyn. It's me."

Evelyn shut her eyes tightly, then reopened them. She moaned faintly. "Hi."

Samona's eyes misted. "What a way to get my attention."

A chuckle came from Evelyn's throat; her mouth hardly moved. "I told you I wanted to see you."

"Next time, kidnap me or something, will you? But don't scare me like this again."

"Okay."

"How do you feel?"

"Not good. But I'm alive."

"Yeah," Samona said softly. "Thank God." She squeezed Evelyn's hand.

"Where's Mark?"

"He's behind me on the chair. Sleeping. Do you want me to wake him?"

"No. Let him sleep."

They fell into silence, and after a long while, Evelyn spoke. "I'm glad you're here."

"I wouldn't be anywhere else."

A soft sob escaped Evelyn's mouth and a tear fell down her cheek. "This isn't what I had in mind, but if it got you here . . ."

"Don't say that."

"You know what I mean. I'm sorry, Samona. Sorry for everything. Sorry about falling for Mark."

"He's the perfect man for you. I know that now."

"But I hurt you."

"We don't have to talk about this now."

Evelyn nodded with difficulty. "Yes. I want to." She swallowed. "If I hadn't been jealous of you, I probably wouldn't have gone after Mark."

"Jealous?"

"Mmm hmm. You know—you were the pretty one. The apple of Daddy's eye."

"Yeah right. You were the apple of Daddy's eye. As far as he was concerned, you could do no wrong."

"Yeah, I got good marks, but so what? I had my head so far in the books I didn't know if I was coming or going. You, on the other hand, enjoyed life. Took chances. Lived on the edge."

"I did not. I was never extreme."

Evelyn huffed. "Remember the time you fell for Sean Garvey?" When Samona groaned and covered her face with a hand, Evelyn continued. "When Mom and Dad didn't want you to see him—they thought you were too young—"

"I was thirteen," Samona interjected, grinning. "I was old enough to have a boyfriend."

"Thirteen and didn't want to listen to anybody. Like you knew everything." Evelyn chuckled. "Remember how angry you got with me when I told Mom and Dad that you were planning to run away?"

Samona sighed wistfully. "Oh yeah. You were Miss Goody Two-Shoes, running off as quickly as you could to get me in trouble."

"That wasn't it. I told myself that was why, but the truth is I was jealous of you. I didn't want to see you having fun when I wasn't. All the guys loved you, but they didn't even notice me."

And that was why Evelyn had pursued Mark. She didn't have to say it; the flash of guilt in her good eye said more than words. Samona swallowed, determined to forget and forgive. None of that mattered now.

"Evelyn, what happened yesterday? Who did this to you?"

"I'd like to know that too." That was Derrick who had spoken. Samona hadn't even heard him return to the room. Now, she faced him. What had happened to her sister was really none of his concern, but she wanted him with her here.

"She tricked me. I thought it was Samona who called my room, so I gave that woman the room number. . . ."

"A woman did this to you?" Derrick asked.

"There were two of them. A man and a woman. Black. They kept asking me about the stolen jewelry."

"Oh God," Samona said. "I'm so sorry, Evelyn. This is all my fault."

"No, it's not," Evelyn said. "I know you had nothing to do with that robbery. But whoever attacked me thinks you did."

"How did they know where you would be?" Derrick asked. "That's what I don't understand. You're in town for one day and they find you?"

Samona's face contorted with guilt. "I think the same people who ransacked my apartment attacked my sister. I had a note by the phone with her name and the hotel where she was going to be staying. . . . God, how could I have been so stupid?"

Derrick touched the back of her neck. "Don't say that. There is no way you could have known—"

"But I should have. I should never have gotten involved with Roger. That's the reason for all of this. If I had just—"

Evelyn reached for Samona's hand and squeezed it. "I don't blame you. Don't blame yourself."

Derrick said, "Listen, you'll have to tell the cops this. I guarantee you, someone will be coming here to ask you questions."

"Maybe not," Samona said. "There are a lot of assaults in Chicago daily. The police don't have time to keep up with everything."

"Trust me, they will," Derrick replied.

"How can you be so sure?"

There he went again, venturing into territory he shouldn't. He lied. "I have a cousin who's a cop. So I know a bit of this stuff."

Samona stood and groaned, folding her arms over her chest.

Evelyn said, "What's wrong?"

"She doesn't like cops," Derrick replied.

"It's not a matter of me not liking cops. It's a matter of them not liking me." She moved to her sister's side again. "Evelyn, I'm not telling you not to talk to them, but maybe you shouldn't tell them what you just told me. About the jewelry bit."

"Because you think that's enough to arrest you?"

Samona shrugged. "I don't know. I only know that the cops have been trying to find a way to connect me to the stolen jewelry for two months. . . ."

"That's—"

"Ridiculous?" Samona supplied. A tiny knot of tension began to tighten in her head. Just moments ago she and her sister were making gains. Now . . .

"I was going to say," Evelyn began slowly, "that I agree

with you. That's something to be concerned about. So, if you don't want me to mention the jewelry, I won't."

Samona drew in a deep breath and let it out in an agitated rush. "I'm sorry, Evelyn. It's just that I'm so stressed."

"There's no need to apologize."

"Thank you," Samona said. "For understanding."

"I don't know." When Samona looked at Derrick, he was shaking his head. "I think it's important to be honest with the police. You want to catch these perps, don't you?"

"Of course," Samona answered.

"Evelyn, you saw them. You have a real lead for the police to follow. If you can identify the people who attacked you, then you can help get them off the street. And from what Samona has told me, I'd bet those people were the accomplices in the robbery and murder—the police need to know this." Derrick cupped Samona's chin. "This may just help you clear your name, Samona."

And he suddenly realized that that's what he was hoping for. For a way to clear Samona's name. Because he cared about her. More than he cared to admit.

"I think he's right, Samona," Evelyn added.

Samona's brain felt like it would explode, thoughts were whirling around in there so fast. She hadn't considered the fact that the ransacking of her apartment, the note and her sister's attack might actually provide proof in her favor. Now, thanks to Derrick, she had another reason to hope. How would she ever repay him for everything he'd done?

"Well?" Derrick asked.

"I think you should write police novels," Samona said.

Caught off guard, Derrick forced a laugh. "Why would you say that?"

"You seem to have a good head for that kind of thing."

Derrick shrugged. "You think so?"

"Yeah. You're a knowledgeable guy."

Evelyn said, "Huh? You've lost me."

"Derrick is a science-fiction writer."

"Not yet published," Derrick interjected.

"Wow. I'm impressed," Evelyn said.

Cocking an eyebrow, Derrick said, "Since you think I sound so 'knowledgeable,' does that mean you'll take my advice?"

Samona half shrugged, half nodded. "Evelyn, if and when the police get here, you tell them what you think is best. I don't know if I'm ready to face them yet, but I am tired of running. I just need some time."

"Fair enough," Evelyn agreed.

Derrick rubbed her back. "You've made the right decision."

Samona faced Derrick and smiled weakly. He was like a ray of sunshine on a cloudy day. An anchor in a stormy sea. Clichés flooded her mind and she wanted to tell him how she felt, but she didn't dare. Here in this hospital room, it was not the time nor the place to tell him what she was really thinking.

Instead, Samona said softly, "I hope so."

Derrick couldn't remember when he'd ever been on the hot seat to the extent he was when Samona had mentioned that he should write police novels. For a moment, he wondered if she knew. Knew and was baiting him. But if she did, surely she wouldn't want to talk to him. She probably wouldn't want to see his face again.

A hand on his chin, Derrick paced the floor by the pay telephones. At least twice he'd reached for a quarter to call Nick. On Wednesdays, Nick didn't start work until the afternoon. Knowing his friend, he was probably sleeping now.

What point was there in waking Nick when he couldn't truly offer him any solutions, Derrick wondered. What

Derrick really wanted was to come clean with Samona. In his heart, he knew he should. Felt he should before it was too late. Maybe if he told Samona the truth now, he could make her understand.

Before he drove himself crazy, Derrick grabbed a quarter and dropped it into the pay phone's slot. Sherry Burns, Nick's wife of three years, answered the phone almost immediately. "Hey, Sherry. It's Derrick. Is Nick around?"

"I think he's sleeping. Let me—"

"No," Derrick interjected. "It's okay. I'll call back."

"He should be getting up anyway. Just give me a second."

About a minute later, Nick came to the phone. "Lawson. You heard."

"Heard what?"

"About Milano. Isn't that why you're calling?"

"No." He paused, waited. "Well don't keep me in the dark. What happened?"

"His current girlfriend, Misty something-or-other, called 911 last night. From his place."

"Really?"

"Mmm hmm. It seems Angelo Milano got a little rough with Misty last night. When the beat cops arrived, she was terrified."

"Are you telling me Milano was arrested for assault?" Derrick asked.

"Actually, no. When the cops got there, Misty wasn't talking. Nada. Milano said something about an intruder breaking in—that he was in the shower at the time."

"And the 911 call?"

"Again, nada. Misty only said she was being assaulted, but not by whom."

"And Milano was in the shower at the time of the assault." Derrick shook his head and chortled.

"So he says. Apparently, when he heard Misty scream, he ran out of the shower, but the intruder got away. He didn't even get a description. Surprisingly, neither did Misty.''

Time and again, Derrick had seen women change their stories in domestic-abuse situations. They would call 911, but by the time the cops got there, they didn't want their husbands or boyfriends arrested. Some actually pursued charges, but many of those women refused to testify against the men in court. As a cop, it was very frustrating. "Does anybody believe that story?"

"If so, I'll be looking for Santa Claus this Christmas. The problem is, we have nothing on him."

Derrick's palms sweat, his skin felt hot, and adrenaline flowed through his veins like hot lava. It was the way he felt every time he had a strong gut feeling about something. Now, a theory was taking shape in his mind. That theory fit this case like the last few pieces of a puzzle. But he had no proof.

"How's your case going?" Nick asked.

"A lot of interesting twists here too." Derrick told Nick about the attack on Samona's sister. "Somebody wants Samona and is going to great lengths to get her. In the last few days, her apartment has been broken into twice."

"Really?"

"Yep. The first time, her place was trashed. Someone was looking for something. Then, after her sister's attack, she got a note with a dead rose—basically a warning."

"To give up the goods," Nick offered. "So she *is* in this up to her ears."

Derrick paused, considered his words. "She says she isn't."

"You talked to her about this?"

"Yep. She opened up to me, told me the whole thing was her boyfriend's doing. That he left her alive to take the fall."

"And you believe her?"

Not only was Nick a fellow cop, he was one of Derrick's

best friends. He could talk to him. He certainly needed to talk to somebody. "My gut tells me she's telling the truth. Not that I haven't been wrong before. But if you could just hear her talk, you'd hear how genuine she sounds."

"A lot of con artists are very convincing."

"True, but as far as she knows, she has nothing to prove to me."

"Maybe she has a thing for you."

"You're fishing."

"You're a handsome man—not as handsome as me, of course. Maybe she wants to impress you. She can't very well do that by admitting that she's a thief and a murderer."

"Maybe," was all Derrick said.

"You know how much I respect you," Nick said after several seconds. "So, if you have doubts about her guilt, then so do I."

A smile touched Derrick's lips. "Thanks, man."

"Whatever you do, Derrick, do it fast. My gut tells me this whole case is going to blow sky-high real soon."

CHAPTER EIGHTEEN

Derrick's conversation with Nick weighed heavily on his mind, even hours later when he and Samona had returned from the hospital. He had a feeling of foreboding, that something was going to happen, but he wasn't sure what.

It was Samona, he realized. He was worried about her. Had been since the break-in. Would be until this whole situation was resolved.

He had asked Samona if she was going to call the police, but she'd said she needed more time. He hadn't pressured her.

Samona hadn't wanted to go inside the house when they'd returned home. Instead, she'd said she wanted to go for a long, quiet walk. Derrick had offered to accompany her, but she had declined. She said she had a lot of things to think about—alone.

With her gone, Derrick was restless. What if something happened to her on the street? What if the people responsible for her sister's assault attacked *her*? Several times, he had started for the door, determined to find her and bring her home, but something had stopped him. His respect for her privacy. And the thought that he should distance himself from her before he became too attached.

Derrick chuckled sarcastically at that thought. It was way too late for that.

There was a knock on his door. *Samona.* Springing from the armchair, Derrick hurried and opened it.

"Oh hello, Mr. Writer." Mrs. Jefferson stood smiling, her arms crossed over her chest. "Sorry to bother you. But I was hoping you could help me with something. A danged thingy has blown. I have no power in my bedroom, bathroom and kitchen, and I'm no good at looking at that box in the basement. You know the one . . ." She snapped her fingers as she tried to find the word.

"The fuse box," Derrick supplied.

"Yes, that's it. Can you help me?"

"Of course, Mrs. Jefferson. Do you have a flashlight?"

"Right here." She pulled one from the waistband of her polyester pants.

"Great." Derrick's smile was forced.

As Derrick and Mrs. Jefferson made their way to the basement, a strange feeling crept over him. He wondered if the fuse had blown naturally, or if someone had tampered with it.

Samona hugged her elbows as a shiver passed over her. Though it was now dusk, the late spring evening was still warm. She wondered why she was cold.

It was a premonition, she realized. A premonition that something was going to happen.

She quickened her pace. How long had she been out? Glancing at her watch, she saw that she had been walking for more than an hour. Turning down a tree-lined street, she headed for home.

The feeling—what was it? It seemed to grow stronger.

Samona stopped and jogged in one spot, trying to shake it off. It wouldn't go away.

She thought of her sister, but felt no anxiety where she was concerned. She thought of Derrick. He certainly couldn't be the cause of her worries. He made her feel things other than anxiety. Sweet sensations she hadn't experienced in a long, long time.

As she turned yet another corner onto another peaceful street, she realized what was bothering her. It was the thought of going home.

Home. She wanted to go home. Not to the house in Oak Park that had become her temporary refuge for these last few weeks. She wanted to go to her house in River Forest. She wanted her life back—her job, her home, her freedom.

She was tired of running. Tired of having to run. Tired of being afraid. Tired of wondering what would happen from one day to the next. She wanted the cloud that had hung over her head for the past two months to be replaced by a ray of sunshine.

She wanted to fight to regain what was hers, but she didn't know where to start. Maybe Derrick was right. Maybe she should go to the police with the information she had. Maybe they would believe her.

But what if they didn't? The prospect of spending the rest of her life in jail was not a pretty one. She'd never survive. Not if she didn't have a hope of ever being set free.

Why did Roger have to go and get himself killed? He was the one person who could prove her innocence. *I need you, Roger.*

A car slowed near her, and Samona's heart leaped to her throat as fear seized her. But the car drove past her. Its occupant seemed to be looking for an address.

Her nerves were frayed. The slightest sound made her jump. She was always on edge because her whole life was a mess.

Why was she thinking like this, she wondered. Her sister was going to recover nicely; she should be happy. But for some reason, she wasn't.

Derrick. It was like someone whispered his name into her ear. She sighed. Yes, she was worried about Derrick. Worried about where their relationship would go. If it could go anywhere.

She hadn't wanted to ask him when he was leaving town, but she knew he wouldn't be sticking around forever. He had a life to return to. So did she. His life was in Toronto. Hers was here. They hadn't known each other long, but if he asked her to move to Toronto with him, the way she felt now, she would say yes. If . . . That was a pretty big if, considering she didn't really know how he felt about her. She only knew she was in love with him.

She thought he was attracted to her. But she'd also thought that Mark would love her forever. She wasn't crying over what was; rather, she was concerned that she didn't really know anything when it came to love. Look how badly she'd screwed up where Roger was concerned.

She couldn't afford to make another mistake. As it was, she'd made two doozies. If she made another one . . .

The sun was setting fast and Samona realized that she had stayed away too long. She'd been so caught up in her thoughts. Now, she wanted to get home to Derrick. What did she have to lose by telling him how she felt?

"There you go, Mrs. Jefferson," Derrick said. Standing, he brushed the dust off his jeans. What he thought would be a ten-minute job had turned into a forty-five minute marathon of chores. He could now add another title to his list of professions: handyman.

He had replaced the burned-out fuse in the basement, filled in a few large cracks in the wall, boarded up a window that for some reason wouldn't lock and now he had just finished screwing in the hinge on a cupboard door. One thing about old houses—it was important to maintain them. Otherwise they would crumble around you.

"I've gotten to everything you've asked me."

"Bless your heart, Derrick. I know I let some of this stuff stay way too long, but I don't know too much about these things."

Derrick nodded. He doubted Mrs. Jefferson knew anything about repairing a home. She seemed more interested in talk shows and tabloids. A man had probably taken care of the handyman responsibilities in the past. She wore a ring so he knew she was married. He wondered what had happened to her husband, but didn't dare ask. He wanted to escape while the night was young.

"Remember to call a carpenter as soon as possible. You really should have that deck's railing fixed."

"I will. Thank you so much." She yawned. "It sure is handy having a man around the house. At times like these, I really miss Arthur."

For a fleeting moment, Derrick thought he would miss this place when he left. Mrs. Jefferson would probably miss him and Samona. She may be a little eccentric, but she was a nice woman who was no doubt lonely.

"You're welcome," Derrick said. "I'll see you."

"Happy writing." Mrs. Jefferson smiled, then yawned again.

"Night."

Mrs. Jefferson watched him retreat, then closed the door. Derrick slowly climbed the stairs, thinking that he'd gotten in a good workout today without having gone to the gym. Bringing his nose to an underarm, he sniffed then grimaced.

A shower was the first order of business when he got to his apartment.

* * *

Samona frowned at Derrick's door when he didn't answer. Where was he? Straining to listen for sound, she thought she heard the shower.

For a moment, she was tempted to go inside and drape herself on his bed, then watch his reaction as he came from the shower and saw her. That would tell her whether or not Derrick was really interested in her.

Giggling at the thought, Samona decided she didn't want to give the man heart failure. She headed for the stairs and the back porch, not yet ready to face her own apartment.

Derrick opened the door to the back porch and watched as Samona whirled around, startled. Her eyes were wide, her lips were slightly parted, and tendrils of her dark, silky hair partly obscured an eye. His throat tightened. Man, she was beautiful.

He stopped in the doorway. "Samona, I didn't realize you were down here." That was a lie. He'd seen her from his window. "I'll leave you to your thoughts."

"No," she said quickly. There was a curious spark in the eye he could see as it met and held his. She let her gaze fall, then turned and faced the railing. Clinging to it with both hands, she looked at him over a shoulder. "I'd like you to stay with me."

"Okay," Derrick said, approaching her. There was something about her tonight. Something electric. He wondered if she was trying to seduce him. Cocking a hip against the railing, he asked, "Have you made a decision yet?"

"About calling the police? No. But I will soon." She paused, pinned him with a level stare. "Why are you so nice to me?"

"Why?" Derrick repeated, buying time to think of an answer. "Because I . . . like you."

She narrowed her eyes speculatively. "Hmm."

"Hmm? What does that mean?"

"Nothing." She leaned back on her heels, supporting her body weight with the railing.

"Whoa," Derrick said, placing a hand on her back. "Be careful. The railing is loose."

She stood tall. "Oh. Thanks. So, Mr. Cunningham, what brings you down here? Writer's block?"

"Actually, yeah."

"Because of me?"

"No . . . why would you say that?"

"Because you've spent so much time taking care of me recently. Being there for me. That must have thrown a wrench in your writing routine."

"A little," Derrick said softly. "But I'm not complaining. There are times when the real world is much more alluring than the fictional ones I create."

Was he saying she was alluring?

Derrick placed both hands on the railing and looked up at the sky. "Like tonight. It's much too beautiful a night to spend it inside."

"I know what you mean." Samona gazed up at the dark sky, sprinkled with golden stars. She would have to do a watercolor of the image soon. The stars were like rays of hope in a dark world. She wished she could reach out and snatch one, capture some of the magic she imagined they held.

"They're beautiful, aren't they?"

Derrick's words startled her out of the enchantment. "Yes. When I look at the sky, I see a large canvas." She gestured with her hands. "I would love to capture the beauty on paper. But I guess when you look at the stars, you see fictional worlds."

Derrick nodded. "Yes. Sometimes. But sometimes I just see it for what it is. A wonder of nature."

Samona nodded absently.

He was behind her now, so close she could feel the heat of his breath in her hair. A wave of longing passed over her and she shuddered.

"No matter how dark your world may seem now, a new day will dawn. You will have brighter days."

His soft words offered her more comfort than she realized she needed at the moment. And he seemed so sincere, the words meant so much.

Derrick's arms slipped through hers and landed on the railing next to her hands. Her skin prickled with excitement. She should turn and face him, slip her arms around his neck, press her lips to his throat. But she didn't dare move.

"Pick a star."

"Hmm?"

"Pick a star. Any star. Then make a wish."

Samona exhaled a shaky breath. A wish. Did she dare?

"Go on," Derrick urged. "Did you pick one?"

"Yes."

"Now close your eyes."

She felt safe with him, and closer to him right now than she'd felt to anyone ever before. Following his instructions, Samona closed her eyes. "Okay. My eyes are closed."

"Go ahead. Make a wish."

Samona paused, held her breath. Then made a wish. She wished for freedom. The freedom to live her life as a whole person. The freedom to love and be loved.

Derrick pressed his lips to the back of her head. The warmest sensation washed over Samona. And the feeling that her wish had come true.

Slowly, she turned around and faced him. Looked up at him from lowered lids. She looked at his firm, squared jaw, then his lips. They were full and tempting and sexy.

Her gaze passed his slim nose and met his eyes. Such intense eyes. The look she saw there was unmistakable. He wanted her.

They were drawn together like a magnet. His lips captured hers in a mind-numbing kiss. Everything—all thoughts of her problems, of her sister, of her foolish choices with men—fled her mind. She could only think of here, of now, of Derrick.

His musky scent consumed her, more powerful than any drug. She was lost in his kiss. His wide palm splayed across her back, his fingertips gently probing. Slowly, Samona's hands found his body. One found his hard, brawny chest; the other found the back of his neck and played with the short hairs on his nape.

Derrick groaned. She moaned. Her fingers explored the width of his chest, the firm muscular pecks, the groove between them, his rapid heartbeat. Finding a flat nipple, Samona gently stroked then tweaked it.

This had to be heaven on earth, Derrick thought as his body reveled in the thousands of exquisite sensations Samona's touch made him feel. He trailed his fingers down her back, over her shoulder blades, her bra straps, down to her waist. Never had he wanted a woman the way he wanted Samona. Deep down, he knew this was wrong, that he was breaching his trust as a police officer. But not even the image of an angry Captain Boyle could stop him now.

He slipped a hand around to the front of her body. He felt her sharp intake of breath when he cupped one full breast. Brushing his thumb over her breast, he could feel the outline of lace, wanted to free her body from it. He deepened the kiss, his tongue delving into her mouth desperately. He tweaked her nipple until it became a hardened peak through the fabric of her bra and shirt.

He wanted her. Right here. Wanted her with a passion that rocked him to the core of his being. His groin felt like it was on fire.

Breaking the kiss he said, "Stay with me tonight, Samona."

Her eyes were dark pools of passion when she looked at him. "With you as in you on the sofa, me on the bed—"

"As in *with* me. With both of us on the bed, or the couch or the kitchen counter for that matter." Her nervous giggle eased the tension. Derrick kissed her nose. "I don't care where. I just want to be with you. I've never wanted anything more in my entire life."

And that was true. He may regret this in the morning, but right now he didn't care.

"Yes, Derrick. Yes."

He kissed her once more, a long, hard, insistent kiss. Then scooped her into his arms. As he carried her through the door and up the stairs, Samona framed his face, kissed his forehead, nestled her nose against his ear. Giggled when she learned he was ticklish behind the ear. She knew that Derrick would fill her days with laughter. Maybe even her nights.

That night, Samona gave and received more love than she had ever known. Derrick took her to a place where time was suspended, where only they existed. He took her to place of magic, laughter and love.

Hours after making love, Derrick couldn't sleep. Thoughts of the woman in his arms, of the profound experience they had shared, kept him awake. Making love to Samona had, quite simply, been the best experience of his life. Better than the day he'd met his new niece. Better even than the moment he'd learned Whitney was safe from danger. Better than anything he could have imagined.

Derrick snuggled against Samona's naked body, planting a soft kiss on her hair. Her hair smelled of apples. Her body felt like velvet against his. Her soft curves molded perfectly against him. They were a perfect fit.

She lay sleeping, the steady rhythm of her breathing like music to his ears. What sound was more beautiful?

Maybe only the sound of his name on her lips in the throes of passion.

Derrick slipped a hand around her small waist, pulling her close. She murmured and placed a hand on his, shifting against him like they had fallen into this position a million times.

This was perfect. Derrick had found a piece of paradise.

As he closed his eyes and savored the sweet feeling, he prayed the morning would never come.

CHAPTER NINETEEN

Alive. That's how Samona felt this morning. So incredibly alive, her heart incredibly full. Derrick had an arm possessively draped around her body, but his shallow, even breathing told her he was sleeping.

She wanted to stay like this forever, but couldn't. There were things she had to do today, like go to the police and hope they believed her story. It was time. Roger was dead and it was up to her to clear her own name. Derrick had given her the strength to pursue this.

Carefully, she slipped from beneath his arm and crawled off the bed. It squeaked in protest, but Derrick didn't move. He was out cold. Samona smiled to herself. She had tired him out.

For a long while, Samona watched him sleep. The edges of his mouth were curled in a grin. He seemed happy. She was happy too. Her eyes roamed the outline of his strong legs beneath the white cotton sheets. The blanket came to his waist. His chest—his beautiful, muscular chest—was bare and exposed. He had no chest hair, but sprinkles of dark curls began near his belly button and went intriguingly lower.

Samona should sketch him. Just as he was now. Maybe, once they were totally comfortable with each other, he would let her do a nude of him. He had a perfect body for clay sculpting.

She whirled around and faced the window. She shouldn't be thinking of tomorrow. Not until she had today figured out. If only she could suspend time, she'd climb back into bed with Derrick and wake him up with a slow, sensual kiss.

The possibilities were endless, once she had today figured out. Picking up Derrick's discarded T-shirt, she slipped it on. It hung to her mid-thigh. He continued sleeping peacefully even as she walked out of the room.

In the kitchen, she searched for tea. He had only packets of instant cappuccino. She wasn't much of an instant coffee drinker, but right now she didn't care. She'd drink instant coffee for the rest of her life—as long as that life included Derrick.

She hoped, prayed, she hadn't made a mistake. Hoped Derrick wasn't the type of guy who only wanted to get in her pants. She doubted that. There was something magnetic between them, something strong. Something real. Samona was sure of that.

She fixed herself a cup of cappuccino, then settled onto the sofa in Derrick's living room. Stretching her feet out, she looked at her toes. Plain. Boring. She would have to add some color. Maybe red.

This change in her was because of Derrick. And it felt good. She could see the silver lining on the cloud that hung over her.

Love. Love had changed her.

She sipped her cappuccino and sighed. Maybe she was getting too excited too soon. Derrick may feel something for her, but she certainly didn't know if he was in love with her. He made her feel special, he made her laugh, he'd given her hope. Yet in some ways he was still an enigma to her.

She didn't really know him.

Samona downed the remaining warm liquid and rose. She pulled the edge of Derrick's shirt to her nose and took a good whiff, inhaling the musky scent that was his alone. Like a giddy schoolgirl, she twirled. Then giggled. She was being totally ridiculous. But being in love had never felt so good.

She wanted to get to know him better. She strolled the living room, but that didn't give her a good idea of who he was. Not even his laptop was here any longer.

She could wake him and ask him everything she wanted to know. Like how old he was. Like what he did to pay the bills while pursuing his writing career. She knew from his body and eating habits that he liked to exercise. Did he work out at a gym or run or mountain climb? Did he have any other passions? Anything crazy like parachuting or hang gliding?

No, she'd let him sleep. After last night, he was tired. But that didn't mean she couldn't look around.

Like her apartment, Derrick's had two bedrooms. Maybe he was using the second one as his office. She arched a brow, intrigued. Maybe his manuscript was in there. She shouldn't snoop, but what would it hurt? It would certainly give her insight into an aspect of Derrick she hardly knew about.

Her hand clasped the brass doorknob. Casting a quick glance at Derrick's bedroom door, she confirmed that he was still sleeping. She would be in and out in just a minute. She'd only peek at his work.

The room was cool, but at least the floor was carpeted. It was a small room with three bookshelves filled with old volumes. Samona scanned the titles on the shelves. They were old classics. Shakespeare, Dickens, Bronte and many others. None of which were Derrick's, she suspected.

Tiptoeing, Samona made her way across the floor to the desk where his computer lay. The laptop was open, but the power was off. Several file folders surrounded the computer, and Samona's hand fell to one. These were probably his notes on his story, or maybe even some of his writing in long hand. He always took a notebook to the beach.

"Last chance to save your integrity and respect his privacy." In defiance of her words, her hand opened the folder.

Instantly, the smile on her lips died and her nerves danced like termites on speed. There was a black-and-white picture of her, one she didn't remember taking. In fact, she hadn't posed for that picture. It was when her hair was still braided. How would Derrick have gotten a picture of her then, when at the time she hadn't known him?

She flipped through the file, fear spreading through her veins like liquid ice. *No, please,* she thought, wondering for a moment if Derrick could be the person who wanted to hurt her. The one who was after the stupid jewelry she didn't have.

There were more pictures. Some color. Some black-and-white. All, of her when she'd had braids.

She dropped that file and picked up another. On the first page was written SAMONA GRAY FILE. A file? What kind of file? As she scanned the pages, the walls felt like they were closing in on her. She saw words like *suspect, investigation, made contact.* Everything else was a blur as she tried to make sense of it all.

"Samona."

She jumped about a foot when Derrick called her name. When she looked at him, his eyes were dark and intense as they bored into her. His face was contorted, but she couldn't read his expression. She didn't know if she should stay or flee. She knew only one thing: Derrick had lied to her.

Somehow, despite the fact that she was trembling, she managed to find a voice to ask, "Who are you?"

If the floor could open and swallow him right now, Derrick would have willed that to happen. Nothing had ever hurt him more than the look of pain and betrayal in Samona's eyes right now. God, he'd never meant to hurt her.

"Who are you?" she repeated, her voice a terrified whisper.

Derrick threw his head back. Closed his eyes. Then faced her and said softly, "I'm a cop."

Her eyes bulged. "A . . ." Her face twitched. "A cop?"

"Yes."

"Oh God."

He wished she would yell at him, charge at him and slap him. Anything but stand there looking absolutely crushed.

Derrick tried to swallow, but his throat was too dry and tight. He felt like a total, complete, certified idiot.

All his life he'd prided himself on honesty. He believed in telling the truth; he didn't believe in deceiving people. Yet he had deceived Samona. Deceived her because of the oath he'd taken to his job.

"Samona, I—"

"No. No. Don't say anything." She seemed to be both thinking and fighting off tears at the same time. She wouldn't look at him. Then suddenly, with a cry of despair, she stormed past him and into the hallway. He followed her but she ran into his bedroom and closed the door. Less than a minute later she appeared, dressed in her T-shirt and shorts. He stood, helpless, speechless. He didn't know what to say or do to undo the damage.

She scurried past him as though he was not even in the

hallway. Watching her, it felt like somebody was literally squeezing the life out of his heart. Seconds later, she was at the door. Then she was gone.

Derrick ran to the door and flung it open. "Samona," he called. *Let me explain,* he added silently. The only response was the sound of pounding footsteps as Samona ran down the stairs. Away from him. Out of his life.

CHAPTER TWENTY

Air. Samona needed air. She gulped to suck in as much oxygen as possible, but her lungs would only allow precious little bits at a time.

"I'm a cop." Derrick's words echoed in her brain over and over, taunting her.

Everything had been a lie. He was a cop. How he must be laughing at her now. He'd certainly gotten her to trust him. She'd even slept with him. She'd talked to him about the robbery. About how the police were trying to find enough evidence to arrest her. And all the while, he'd been the police. He'd been the enemy.

She was more than a fool. She was gullible, stupid. Why had she gone against her better judgment and started a relationship with Derrick? First Mark, then Roger, now Derrick—she was through with men. For some reason, she was cursed where they were concerned.

Samona hustled on the pavement, part jogging, part speed-walking as she put as much distance between herself and Derrick as humanly possible. He had called her name as she charged down the stairs, but she hadn't stopped.

"I'm a cop."

She should have known. By the little things he said and did. Good grief, she'd suggested he write cop novels. Deep down a part of her must have known. So why had she so easily been seduced?

God, how could she have been such a fool—again? She was doomed when it came to men. She always chose the wrong ones—men who betrayed her.

Derrick had probably called the station already and the police would track her down on the street like an animal. A nasty lump formed in her throat as she realized the depth of his betrayal. How he'd met her, how he'd smiled at her, all those sweet, encouraging things he said—all lies.

All so that he could lock her in jail and throw way the key.

She'd never meant a thing to him. Not even when they'd made love. A tear trickled down her face. Even the lovemaking had been a lie.

If the police found her, she wouldn't resist arrest. Running would only delay the inevitable. If she was going to spend the rest of her life in jail, what difference would it make if that day came now?

Derrick slammed an open palm against the wall. Cursed. Cursed again. Samona had run out of here so fast she forgot her purse. He should be happy; she was in no condition to drive. But he wasn't. Wasn't because Samona was in danger alone on the street.

After she had taken off, Derrick had run downstairs to her apartment, hoping to find her there, but she wasn't. By the time he made it to the street, she was nowhere in sight though her car was parked in the driveway.

He would have to call the station before he went after her. Let Captain Boyle know that he had blown the assignment. He wasn't looking forward to this, but he may as well get it over with. All he really cared about now was Samona.

He picked up the receiver and called Captain Boyle. "Captain," he said when the man answered the phone. "It's Lawson. I've got a problem. A big one."

"What kind of problem?" Already, the captain sounded none too pleased.

"My cover's been blown," Derrick said into the receiver, deceptively calmer than he actually felt.

"What?!"

Grimacing, Derrick put the receiver to his other ear.

"How the hell did that happen?"

"I can't explain now. What's important now, sir, is that Samona has taken off, and I have reason to fear for her safety. Sir, I believe she's innocent."

"You find her and bring her in!"

"Yes, sir."

Derrick hung up and grabbed his car keys from the kitchen table. His conversation with Captain Boyle had been brief, and he wondered how angry the captain really was, especially with his statement that he believed Samona was innocent. Hurrying through the door, Derrick acknowledged that right now, it didn't really matter. It only mattered that Samona was out on the street, alone. It mattered that he had a nagging feeling, telling him he was too late.

It mattered that he cared for her.

Samona angrily brushed away the tears that wet her cheeks. She didn't want to cry, certainly not over a man who wasn't worth her tears. Derrick had betrayed her and she had to remember that.

But every time she thought about the betrayal, her eyes filled with tears once again. What hurt was that she had started to care about him. Crossing the street, she quickened her pace. Who was she kidding? She was in love with him. Had been probably since their first dinner date—the pizza in his apartment.

A sucker—that's what she was. Her heart ached even more because Derrick had hurt her the most. Certainly more than Mark ever had, and he'd dumped her for her sister. At the time, she'd thought that was bad. But Derrick's betrayal topped that. Because she'd cared more about him than any other man. And now to discover that his feelings had all been a lie . . .

Maybe there was something about her that made men want to hurt her, betray her. How else could she explain three bad relationships in her life? She hadn't really cared for Roger, and until Derrick, she hadn't known what love was. Not really. Mark had been special in some ways, but now she knew that she'd only been infatuated with him— not in love with him.

She loved Derrick.

She bit down hard on her lip and squeezed her eyes shut, willing herself to forget that Derrick even existed. Somehow, she had to forget him.

Samona didn't notice that the car next to her was slowing. She didn't have time to scream as a hand came down around her mouth. Without much effort, she was dragged into the dark-colored sedan. Then, with only a dog barking in protest, the car drove down the tranquil street, unnoticed.

CHAPTER
TWENTY-ONE

Samona squirmed. Tugged. Tried to pull her hands and feet free of the ropes that bound her.

"Relax," the woman said. "We're almost there."

It was hard to breathe with the gag. She tried not to panic, but bile rose in her throat and she choked. *Breathe,* she told herself. If she had a panic attack now, she'd suffocate. She tried as hard as she could to breathe evenly through her nose.

"Shut her up," the man said.

"She ain't hurting nobody."

"I can't concentrate with her freakin' out like that. Shut her the hell up."

Samona's eyes darted to the woman in terror. She tried to beg for her life, but couldn't do anything but moan and groan because of the gag.

A false smile on her lips, the woman who sat beside her slipped an arm around her neck. "Don't worry, honey. This won't hurt a bit."

* * *

"Please let her be home," Derrick said as he descended the steps to the second floor. Though he knew it was unlikely, he hoped she had returned. Now more than ever, he knew her safety depended on it.

When Derrick's feet landed on the second level, he saw someone at Samona's door. A man dressed in dark, baggy clothes. He was about his height and his complexion, but a baseball cap hid his features. As soon as the man saw him, he tore off, sprinting down the steps.

"Hey!" Derrick yelled. That side profile. . .The man looked strangely familiar.

Roger!

Derrick sped after him like the devil himself chased him. His long legs carried him quickly. On the street, Roger was almost in a car. Derrick charged after him and caught the door before it closed. Roger rammed the key in the ignition and tried to start the car, but Derrick grabbed him and forced him out of the car before he could.

"Police officer! Don't move!" Derrick pinned him to the asphalt.

Roger groaned, then swore.

"Hands behind your back!"

Roger didn't put up a fight. Clearly, he'd been through the routine before. Behind his back, he crossed his arms at the wrists.

Derrick's heart raced with excitement. Roger was the key to finding Samona. Securing Roger's wrists, he heaved him off the ground. "You're under arrest, pal."

"Start talking." Derrick stood above Roger, who sat in the armchair in his living room.

"Not until I get to speak to a lawyer."

"There's no time for a lawyer. Samona—you remember

her—the one you left to take the fall for a crime you committed." As Derrick said the words, he knew it was true. Had known it all along. What he didn't know was what Samona ever saw in Roger. He pushed that thought aside.

"I have nothing to say."

Derrick placed a hand on each armrest, facing Roger head-on. "Roger, we can do this the easy way, or the hard way. You can either start talking, or I can call for a car to take you to the station and you can talk there. But I guarantee you, the other cops, they won't be near as nice as I am. Everybody's sick of this case—and they've been itching to get someone real bad." He cocked an eyebrow. "If I hand you to them on a silver platter, you'll be like fresh meat to men who haven't eaten in months."

Roger squirmed. His tough facade was fading. "I'll take my chances."

"Will you? And are you willing to gamble with Samona's life, you spineless shell of a man?" Disgusted, Derrick stood and scowled.

Roger blew out an anxious breath. Derrick waited. Nothing. Finally Derrick said, "Tell me this—what brought you here? Back to Chicago? To Samona's place?"

"I got a call. I was told that Samona was here. I was also told a few other things that I won't repeat right now. I came here to check out if what I heard was true."

"Stop the riddles."

"Can I ask you a question?" When Derrick nodded, Roger asked, "Where is she?"

"Samona . . . left . . . a while ago. When I went to look for her, she wasn't anywhere in the neighborhood."

"Damn."

"What? Do you know something?"

"Someone told me that he'd take her—"

"Who?"

"Someone. Someone I owe. I was hoping that I would get to her first."

"To finish her off?"

"No, I—I cared about her. I wanted to warn her."

Derrick paced the floor in front of Roger. "You know," he began, facing the thug, "I don't know what points you think you'll gain by keeping tight-lipped. Maybe—maybe—if you come clean and help save Samona, *that* will earn you some points. But if you don't, and something happens to her . . ."

"All right." Roger buried his face in his hands. "Jeez." He mumbled something Derrick couldn't hear. "Okay."

"Who has Samona?"

"A guy named Alex Reilly."

Derrick nodded. He knew the name. Alex was one of Chicago's known criminals. "AKA Red."

"He and I . . . we both did that hit on Milano's store. Red's pissed 'cause I cheated him. We were supposed to split the jewels but I took off with everything."

"And faked your death."

"Yeah."

"So why come back? Everyone thought you were dead—you were home free."

"I shouldn't say anything else without my lawyer."

Precious time was wasting and Derrick's nerves were raw. "All right. That's it." He grabbed Roger by the collar. "We're going to the station. Not even your lawyer can get you off Murder One charges."

Roger threw his hands in the air. "Look, I didn't kill that woman, okay?"

"Don't you dare pin this on Samona."

"I'm not! Red took her out. That's why he's so pissed—he took her out and he didn't even get the payoff."

Derrick eyed Roger carefully. His nape prickled. What he'd just said implied something more than just a random robbery. "What do you mean the 'payoff'? Payoff as in the jewelry?"

"I mean the payoff for taking her out."

"Someone hired you to kill Sophia Milano." The words came out as a statement even though it was a question. God Almighty, it was all making sense.

"Jeez. We did this and we're not even going to get the money . . ."

Derrick looked Roger squarely in the eye. "Who hired you?"

"The woman's old man. Mr. Milano."

Her head hurt like the devil and she was groggy. Groaning softly, Samona tried to open her eyes. Tried to and couldn't. It took her only a second to realize that she was blindfolded.

Immediately, Samona remembered being abducted, bound and gagged. Her heart raced. She already knew what her abductors looked like, so why had they blindfolded her? There was only one thing she could think of: they didn't want her to see when they were going to kill her.

As terror seized her, her breathing turned ragged. Her nostrils burned as she inhaled and exhaled hastily. *Stop it,* she told herself. Desperately, she tried to control her panic. She wouldn't die like this—couldn't. From somewhere she got strength—strength to control her fear if even for a few minutes. How much more of this she could take, she didn't know.

She could hear angry voices. The man and woman from the car. Since she couldn't see, all Samona's other senses were heightened. She could feel the dust in the air cling to the perspiration on her skin. She could feel the tension in the room, and that made her worry. Something wasn't going as planned. She could hear the fear in her captors' voices. She could smell death in the air.

Never had she ever been so scared. Not even when Roger had put a gun to her head. Then, she couldn't bring herself to believe that he would actually shoot her. But she didn't know these two. They'd brutally beaten her sister just to send a message. God only knew what they would do to her.

Every sound, every footstep on the floor made her jump. Because each moment could be her last. *Please God,* she silently prayed, *protect me. Don't let me panic. Don't let me give up hope.*

Hope. Derrick had been the one to make her hope again. The thought of him and his betrayal brought fresh tears to her eyes, but she fought them. Fought them because they had nowhere to go, and beneath the blindfold, the tears only made her eyes sting.

The angry voices grew louder and clearer. "He'll come. He's got a soft spot for her . . ."

"It's been three hours," the female said. "Where is he? I told you this wasn't a good idea—"

"Give him time."

As footsteps neared her, Samona froze. This could be it, the end. Cold, rough fingers stroked her cheek and her heart felt like it would burst in her chest.

The man said coolly, "If he knows what's good for him, he'll be here."

Then he walked away chuckling, leaving Samona shaken and terrified.

Derrick had just spoken to Captain Boyle and relayed the news Roger had told him. Given Roger's evidence, some officers were on their way to arrest Angelo Milano on probable cause. Some were en route to join Derrick with both cruisers and plain cars. With Roger as their guide, they would search Alex Reilly's hideouts in an attempt to find Samona.

If anything happened to her, Derrick would never forgive himself. Closing his eyes, he prayed it was not too late.

When Mr. Milano opened the door and saw three uniformed police officers on his porch, his lips thinned with concern. "Officers, what's going on? Have you arrested my wife's murderer?"

"Angelo Milano," one officer said, "you are being placed under arrest for the murder of your wife."

"What?" His eyes widened in angry indignation.

"You have the right to remain silent—"

"This is crazy," Angelo yelled as he was placed in handcuffs. "You don't know what you're talking about."

The officers continued anyway, ignoring his protests. By the time he was brought to a cruiser at the curb, a small crowd of onlookers had gathered. His neighbors. The people who knew and respected him. They were all there to witness his demise.

Suddenly, this all became real. As Angelo was being placed in the cruiser's backseat, he burst into tears.

Samona drifted in and out of consciousness. It was easier to sleep, to forget the pain, although something told her she should fight to stay awake.

She didn't want to stay awake. Awake, her mind drifted to Derrick, his betrayal and the insufferable pain in her heart. Would she ever get over this?

She should have known better, but she was through kicking herself. What mattered was that she had given her heart, totally and completely, to a man she didn't even know. If she ever made it out of here, she would never make that same mistake again.

Oh, Derrick, why? New tears filled her eyes.

Think of his betrayal, she told herself, willing herself not to cry. *Find your anger and get over him.*

She wished it were so easy. This time, she didn't know if she would ever find all the pieces of her smashed heart. If she could even find them, she didn't know if she'd be able to put her heart back together. Though she prayed she'd get out of here alive, she sensed after this she'd never truly be alive again. How, after this last heartbreak, could she be anything but emotionally numb?

All because she'd dared to believe in love one last time.

Never again, Samona vowed. If she made it out of here alive, she'd never love again.

CHAPTER
TWENTY-TWO

As each second came and went, more beads of perspiration popped out on Derrick's body. Constantly, he wiped his forehead and adjusted the air conditioning, but his glands were working overtime. After more than four hours of searching, Samona had not been found. He and his team of officers had checked out Alex's residence, an ex-girlfriend's home he apparently frequented and the home of a Chicago gangster whom he was reportedly good friends with. He was at neither place.

"He's gotta be here," Roger said as the plain car Derrick was driving approached a run-down, boarded-up building in Chicago's south side.

"Five-o!" he heard someone yell as the police cars advanced to the curb. Several young men darted down the street in both directions as if their lives depended on it. More young criminals, Derrick thought, shaking his head. Luckily for them, Alex was his concern today.

"What's this place?" Derrick asked. He suspected it was a buy-and-sell shop for illegal narcotics.

"It's a drug spot. You know." Now that Roger knew he might be able to cut a deal with the prosecutor, he was talking nonstop.

"Why didn't you tell us about this in the first place?" Derrick asked, frustrated.

"Because I didn't think of it 'til now."

Derrick rammed the car into park and he, the officer seated next to him and Roger jumped out. He signaled to the other officers and they cautiously approached the building with their guns drawn. Someone ran from the side of the building then, startling Derrick. Adrenaline flowing through his veins, Derrick turned, ready.

It was a young, harried-looking woman carrying a baby. "Don't shoot!" she yelled. "Please . . ."

Turning down the street, she ran off. Derrick blew out a ragged breath. Young kids on drugs, especially mothers, was a sad sight, but one Derrick was familiar with. Drugs needed to be removed from the streets, permanently. They were a poison, slowly killing people in the projects and even in some nicer neighborhoods. That's why he had devoted his time to the drug unit.

After a moment, he said, "Let's go."

He, his officers and Roger walked down the side of the building and approached a door. Looking around in the darkened building, it soon became obvious that it was empty. Remnants of crack pipes littered the ground, along with other debris, indicating that the place had been occupied recently. But the arrival of police cars had scared everybody away.

"The place is empty," an officer called from the dark room.

Derrick growled long and hard, both angry and frustrated. It was already dusk, and the chances of finding Samona alive after all these hours grew less likely.

He turned to Roger. "Think, darn it. Think hard. Where is Alex? You said he left a message for you on the street.

If he wanted you to find him, then you have to know where he is."

"I don't know! We've been to all the places I can think of."

"That's not good enough."

"Okay. Wait. I think I know where he could be."

Derrick faced him with anticipation. "Where?"

"His mom's place."

"With Samona?" Derrick couldn't mask his disappointment.

"It's possible." Roger shrugged.

"All right." It was another lead and Derrick couldn't ignore it. He took a moment to tell his men the next place they would check out, although he wasn't putting much hope in that. Then, climbing into the unmarked cruiser, he said to Roger, "Lead the way."

"Here. Drink this."

The woman had ungagged her and now held a bottle of water to her mouth. As Samona gulped the liquid, she thought it was more precious than gold. Nothing had ever tasted as sweet. Her throat had been so raw and dry she'd thought it would crack.

Samona moaned faintly when the woman pulled the bottle away. She wished she could see. She said, "Please . . . take off this blindfold. I–I can't stand it."

"Really?" That was the man's hard, cold voice. "That's too bad. Babe, gag her."

"No . . . please. I swear I'll be quiet."

She felt a face near hers, could smell foul breath. A finger stroked her face and she jerked away. The man said, "Sorry. You might scream."

"No. I promise, I wouldn't. I won't. . . ."

He said, "I can't take that chance." To his accomplice he said, "Gag her. Now."

"No—" Samona's protest died as her head was jerked back and her mouth forced open. As the gag was replaced, her throat tightened with fear.

"Don't worry," the woman said. "It shouldn't be too long now."

Too long for what? Samona's mind screamed. Deep in her heart, she didn't think she wanted to know.

The trip to Alex's mother's home had only accomplished two things. One, they learned that Samona was not there. Two, they scared Alex's mother. She had let Derrick and his team search her house, but cried the entire time. As Derrick and the other officers left the premises, Ms. Reilly begged them not to shoot her son.

If more children thought of the grief they caused their parents with their criminal activities, Derrick suspected less would get involved in crime. The trouble was, no matter what the crime, no one ever thought they would get caught.

Ms. Reilly would be doing a lot more crying.

This time when Derrick slipped into the cruiser, he dropped his head to the steering wheel. He couldn't give up. Not until he'd found Samona. But his men were getting tired. After several hours, they had no results.

Roger seemed exasperated. From what Derrick could tell, he was being straight with them. He would be going to jail the moment the search ended, so he had nothing to gain by sending them on a wild-goose chase.

An officer approached the driver's side of Derrick's car. Derrick rolled down the window. The officer said, "What now?"

"I don't know," Derrick admitted. "I know you guys are tired, and if you want to take off, I'll understand. But I can't give up. Not yet."

"Don't worry about us, Lawson. We want to get this perp as much as you do. Just name the place and we're there."

Detective Abdo opened the car door and took a seat beside Derrick. "I say we keep going."

Derrick appreciated his colleagues' loyalty. Now, they needed another place to search. Looking at Roger through the rearview mirror he thought that he had pushed him as far as he could, but maybe one last try. One last try before he relieved the other officers and brought Roger to the station. On his own, he would search for Samona until he found her.

"Roger, if there is any other place you know of—*any* place at all—you have to tell me."

Roger frowned. Thought hard. Then, after a long, tension-filled moment, his eyes lit up. "Wait a minute," he said slowly, excitement filling his voice. "I think I know."

Derrick turned and faced him, his heart once again filling with hope. "Where, Roger?"

Roger chortled. "It's gonna sound crazy, but Red is crazy enough—"

"Where?" Derrick asked again. *Let this be the one.*

"Milano Jewelers."

"That place is boarded up," Detective Abdo said.

"Yeah," Roger agreed. "And that's why it's perfect. It's where it all started, and it's where it all will end."

The back of Derrick's neck prickled. It made sense. Good God, it made a lot of sense. To the officer outside his window he said, "Milano Jewelers. That's where she is."

The officer ran off, shouting the next location to be searched to the rest of the team. Quickly everyone scrambled into their cars.

Starting the car, Derrick sped toward River Forest. He knew Samona was there, felt it.

He could only hope he got there in time.

CHAPTER
TWENTY-THREE

She didn't want to give up.

But doubts were starting to creep into her mind.

Where the ropes bound her, her skin was raw and stung each time she moved. Her breathing was shallow but at least even. Her energy was spent. She was exhausted. Shifting in the seat, Samona wondered if this was the way she would die. Here, attached to a chair, would she just fall asleep and never wake up?

Derrick. The thought of him always made her want to cry, but she couldn't cry. She swallowed. Choked on her saliva. Tried desperately not to give up the fight now. A coughing fit could cause her to suffocate. Slowly and deliberately, she regained control of herself. If she got emotional every time she thought of Derrick, he would be the death of her even though he wasn't physically here.

She had to forget him.

He took too much of her energy. Already, she was fading. Again. It was an effort to stay awake and she didn't even know if she wanted to be awake. Awake, she would face her death with fear. Drawing in deep, even breaths, Samona decided not to fight it. With sleep, there was no pain. Only peace.

As her world started to fade, she wondered if she would ever wake up again.

A block away from Milano Jewelers, Derrick stopped his car and killed the lights. The two cruisers behind him did the same. If Alex had Samona at this store—and Derrick prayed Alex did—Derrick wanted to approach unawares. Any sign of cop cars could scare Alex into doing something stupid.

Like kill Samona. If she wasn't already dead.

She wasn't. If she was, he would know it. Feel it. Just as he knew Alex was here.

Derrick and his fellow officers crept down the street to an alley. At the opening of the alley, Derrick instructed some of his men to go to the front of the building while he, Roger and a few other officers went to the back. Alex would not escape.

When they reached the back door of Milano Jewelers, Derrick paused. His heart was pumping so fast he thought it would explode in his chest. Samona was just beyond that door and he was afraid. Afraid that he might be too late. Afraid that something might go wrong. Afraid that if she were alive, she wouldn't want to see him.

He swallowed his fears. It was time to act.

Roger grabbed his arm, and Derrick turned and faced him. "I know Red is in there," he said. "He wants me. Let me go in there alone, talk to him. I'll try to free Samona."

"No way," Derrick said.

"You don't understand. Red always packs a piece. If you go in there, he'll panic. If he hasn't killed Samona already, he probably will. You don't want to risk that."

"He's right," Detective Abdo said.

Derrick gritted his teeth. "Yeah. He has a point."

"So you'll let me go ahead?"

Derrick placed a firm hand on Roger's shoulder. "If this is some kind of setup, so help you God."

"This place is surrounded. I'd be a fool to set you up now. I just want this over with."

"All right," Derrick said. "Be careful."

Derrick and the three officers with him exchanged concerned glances as Roger slipped into the store. His gun was drawn, and he was ready. Derrick prayed he didn't have to use it.

Moments later, a shot rang out in the night. Derrick's heart leaped to his throat. Fear propelled his feet through the back door and he charged inside, followed by the other cops.

The store was dark, softly illuminated by a light from a back room. Immediately, Derrick saw Samona in one corner of the store, gagged. As officers swarmed the store, turning on flashlights and calling out, Derrick ran to her.

Her head lolled forward. Derrick's throat constricted. Good God, was he too late?

"Lawson!" someone shouted. "We've got 'em. Two of them. But Roger has been shot."

Right now, Derrick didn't care about anything but Samona. Frantically, he fumbled with the gag and blindfold, then the ropes that bound her hands and feet. She didn't move, not even when he pulled her into his arms. "No! No, God!"

Officer Smith came to his side. "Lawson, is she okay?"

"I don't know." Derrick pressed his ear to her face, checking for breath. Relief flooded him. "She's breathing."

"An ambulance is on its way," Smith said. "Though it might be too late for Benson."

Derrick barely registered what Officer Smith said.

Lightly, he tapped Samona's face. "Wake up. Come on, Samona."

Her head moved. First she moaned, then coughed. Then bolted upright, flailing her arms in the air. "No!"

Derrick pulled her to him, cuddling her head. "You're okay. Samona, it's me. Derrick."

She stiffened. Then pulled her head back and looked at him. She seemed dazed and afraid.

"It's okay," Derrick said. "It's over."

Samona whimpered. She tried to speak, but her voice came out as a croak.

Derrick didn't know if she understood him so he said, "You're free."

Samona sagged against him. Cried. Derrick held her, his own eyes misting with tears. What if he had been too late? He would never have had the chance to apologize to her. He would never have felt her soft body in his arms again. He would never have been able to tell her he loved her.

Love. The word surprised him. But he knew it was true. He loved her. Somehow, he had to make her understand that he hadn't meant to hurt her. He was only doing his job.

"Samona," Derrick began.

"Shh," she said. "Not now. Please."

"But—"

"Later," she said softly. "Not now."

"Okay."

The store was chaotic, filled with much noise and move-ment as the three people responsible for Mrs. Milano's death were taken into custody. But Derrick didn't notice. All his thoughts were on Samona. The woman in his arms. The woman he knew he loved without a doubt.

* * *

Samona was exhausted, but alive. Alive. Safe.

The night had been harrowing. After being checked out and okayed by the ambulance staff, she had been taken to the police station. For hours, she answered questions for both the police and the media. She had called her sister and Mark and given them the news. Then she had called Jennifer. Jennifer was with her now.

Derrick had saved her. And now, thanks to him, she supposed, she was free. Alex and his accomplice Marie were in custody. Roger, though critically injured from a gunshot wound, was in the hospital and expected to survive.

Alex and Marie had been Roger's accomplices. Roger had robbed the jewelry store and after he had knocked her out, Alex had killed Sophia Milano. It was all part of Mr. Milano's plan. Capitalizing on the previous jewelry store robberies, he had hired Roger to kill his wife and make it look like a robbery gone bad.

It was all so overwhelming. And to think she had been a part of it all—even though an unwilling part—was amazing. She was glad it was over.

Though tired, she had happily posed for pictures. This time when her face made the headlines, it would be as a free woman, not a wanted one.

She was happy.

Jennifer approached her in the small interrogation room, smiling. "You're free to go."

"Great." Never had she been so relieved in her life. Finally, the sun had burst through her gray cloud.

Rising from the chair, she turned to her friend. "Let's go."

Jennifer placed a hand on her arm. "Wait a minute. Aren't you going to say good-bye to Derrick?"

Samona shook her head. She hadn't seen Derrick in hours, not since he had brought Jennifer in to see her.

"I don't think so."

"Why not?"

"Because . . ."

"Because what?"

"Not now," Samona said.

Jennifer folded her arms across her chest. "Because he's a cop. Right?"

"I'm tired. I want to go home."

"You're going to run."

Samona slumped into the chair. "Jen, I'm not running."

"Yes you are."

Samona ran a hand over her hair. "Okay, fine. Maybe I am. But why shouldn't I? He lied to me—"

"He saved your life."

"That's beside the point."

Jennifer raised a skeptical eyebrow. "Is it? I thought that was pretty significant."

"More significant than the fact that he was hoping to arrest me for crime I didn't commit?"

"He was doing his job."

"He lied to me. I can't trust him."

Jennifer dropped into the seat beside Samona. "My God, woman, you are one stubborn person. If you can't see that Derrick is in love with you—"

"Love . . . ? Don't be crazy."

"You're the one who's crazy. That man loves you. It's as plain as day."

Samona made a face. "Yeah right."

"Fine. You should at least give him the chance to explain. Wouldn't you want the same if you were in his shoes?"

"I would never be in his shoes."

"And three months ago, you never would have dreamed that you'd be arrested."

Samona let out a ragged breath. "What's your point?"

"My point is that sometimes things happen beyond our control. Sometimes bad things happen to good people.

Sometimes you get an assignment you hate. But you have to do it."

Samona stood. "Okay, Jen. I hear you. I'll talk to him. But not now. Later."

"Stubborn," Jennifer muttered.

"What was that?" Samona asked.

Jennifer flashed her a syrupy smile. "Nothing. Let's go."

Derrick stared at the phone as if it offered the answers to all his questions. He was confused and wanted someone to talk to. Right now, Whitney was that person. A woman might help him figure out what to do.

Afraid to see Samona, he had locked himself in his office while he worked on his notes. He could have gone home hours ago to his bed where he belonged, but he was too wired to sleep.

Derrick reached for the receiver. Lifting it, he stared at it for several moments. He replaced it. Picked it up again. Finally he slammed it down and groaned.

It was too early to call Whitney. Besides, she couldn't help him. He needed to help himself. He needed to talk to Samona. Hiding behind his desk and his paperwork would not negate that fact.

He stood and stretched. It felt like he had a thousand worms crawling in his stomach, he was so nervous. But he had to talk to Samona. Because he cared and he wanted her to understand.

When he left his office, he searched the entire station. Samona wasn't there. After speaking to another officer, he learned that Samona had been released.

Maybe that was for the best. If she hadn't sought him out to say good-bye, maybe she didn't want to see him. Maybe he should leave well enough alone.

* * *

If she hadn't had her things to pack, Samona would have gone crazy. Jennifer had helped her for a few hours but then had to leave. Of course, Jennifer had given her parting words of advice: talk to Derrick.

Samona couldn't. Not that she didn't want to, but what would that accomplish? Derrick didn't love her. He'd sweet-talked her, made her laugh, and made love to her because it was his job. Because he wanted to get her to confess to a crime she didn't commit.

Their relationship was a lie. What point was there in talking to him? He would go his way and she would go hers—separately.

If it was so simple, then why did it hurt so much? Dropping onto the sofa, Samona acknowledged that she didn't have an answer. Other than the fact that she cared. Cared too much. Even now, she wondered about him.

He hadn't come to see her. Part of her wished he would. The part that was a traitor. The part that had gotten her into trouble in the first place. Still, she couldn't help regretting the fact that she hadn't given Derrick a chance to explain back at the jewelry store.

It was hard to believe that just a couple of nights ago, she and Derrick had made love. Sweet love. For her, it had been a life-changing experience. For the first time in a long time her heart had felt full. Now, it felt empty. Her whole body felt empty, drained.

Stop thinking about Derrick, she told herself. *Forget him. Get up and go on with your life.*

She didn't move. Again, she willed herself to get up, to bring her things to the car. To leave and get on with her life. But she couldn't.

Finally, alone on the sofa, she fell asleep.

* * *

Derrick lifted his hand to knock on Samona's door, but paused. He was sure she didn't want to see him. So why was he here?

Because he had to make her understand. He'd had the entire day to think it over and he knew what he had to do. He faced many difficult situations as a cop, so why this particular situation scared him so much he didn't know.

That was a lie. He did know. He didn't know when or why it had happened, but he had given his heart to Samona. Now, all his hopes and dreams were in her hands. She had the power to hurt him the way no woman ever had.

He couldn't blame her if she did. He would deserve it for what he'd done to her. Still, he couldn't help hoping that she would hear him out and give him a chance.

His hands shook. His nerves were frayed. Closing his eyes, Derrick counted to ten slowly. When he reopened them, he knocked on the door, not giving himself the chance to back away.

When Samona heard the knock, she froze, sat upright and stared at the door. For a moment, she couldn't draw breath.

There was another knock. Her stomach coiled. She should get up, answer the door. But she was afraid. Afraid it wasn't Derrick.

That kind of thinking would get her nowhere. She couldn't stay here on this old sofa for the rest of her life. If it wasn't Derrick at the door, then so be it. She would move on somehow. But she had to stop running.

Slowly, her stomach coiling, Samona rose from the sofa and went to the door. Her hand on the doorknob, she paused briefly. Then, she swung it open.

Derrick had been walking away, but when he heard the door open he turned around and faced her. Her stomach flip-flopped and her heart raced. She wanted to smile. Wanted to run to him. Instead, she stood with her hand on the doorknob, her back stiff, her face blank.

She said, "Derrick."

Slowly, he approached her, wondering what she was thinking. Was her pulse racing the way his was? Did she want to see him? He couldn't tell. Her face was devoid of any emotion. There seemed to be a spark in her eyes, but her lips were pulled into a thin line.

"Uh, Samona. I . . . uh, we didn't get to talk last night."

"I . . . know."

"I was . . . hoping we could . . . now."

"Uh, I see." She shifted on her feet. "Please . . . uh, come in."

Derrick approached her, the heat of his body enveloping hers. She didn't dare move as he passed her and walked into the apartment. Despite her resolve to get on with her life without him, she couldn't stop her heart from hoping.

He had come to her.

She closed the door and stepped into the room. Derrick's gaze was fixated on the Oriental rug. He had a newspaper rolled under his arm.

When she approached him, he spoke. "Uh, this is for you."

Extending both hands, Samona took the newspaper from him. It was the *Chicago Tribune*. On the front page, there was a picture of her, her lips curled in a grin. The caption read: SCHOOLTEACHER CLEARED IN MURDER CASE.

A laugh escaped her throat. Then she ran a hand over her face as she felt the onslaught of tears. It was official. She was free. She had her life back.

Her eyes flew to Derrick's face. He was smiling, though tentatively. "Congratulations," he said.

Samona said softly, "Thank you."

"Now everyone will know you're innocent."

"Yes. Finally." Her voice broke, but she didn't cry. Silence fell between them. Samona crossed her arms, then spoke. "Uh, is that why you came by?"

"Yeah." Derrick nodded. "I didn't know if you had seen the paper."

"I caught a bit of the news."

"So did I. You're quite the celebrity."

"This time in a good way." She stopped her lips from curling, even though she wanted to shout the good news to the world. Wringing her fingers, she averted her eyes.

"How are your hands?"

"Fine," she said quickly. She looked at him. "Just some bad scrapes but I'll get over that."

"So . . . you're okay?"

Samona nodded tightly. "I will be now."

"Good." Derrick pursed his lips and looked at her. She looked away. She didn't want to see him. He should go. "All right." He took a step toward the door.

"Are you leaving?" Samona asked.

Derrick's hand went to the back of his neck. "I . . . I don't want to bother you."

"Oh." She should tell him he wasn't bothering her. She should tell him to stay. Once he walked out that door, he was walking out of her life forever. She knew that.

Derrick took a few more steps, this time passing her. Her lips trembling, Samona didn't turn around. He was leaving her. It was over. She was letting the best thing in her life walk away.

She didn't hear the door. Instead, she heard his footsteps as he approached her again. Derrick said, "Samona, I want to tell you something."

She turned to face him, her pulse pounding in her ears. "Go ahead."

"I want you to know that I knew you weren't guilty. Yes,

I was supposed to investigate you, but I never could bring myself to believe you were involved in the robbery and murder.''

"Why not?" She needed to know.

Because the moment I looked at you, I knew. "I don't know. I just did."

"Then why didn't you end the investigation?"

"Because . . ." His voice trailed off. Softly, he added, "Maybe because I couldn't face the thought of walking away from you."

Samona's stomach lurched. "Hmm."

"I'm sorry. Samona, I know it may not mean much now, but I do hope one day you can bring yourself to forgive me."

"I . . . I don't know. Derrick, you made me . . ."

"What?" He moved toward her, hoping. "What did I make you do?"

"Care," Samona blurted out. "God, I shouldn't have said that. I don't want to make you feel guilty. I know you were doing your job. . . ."

"Is that what you think? That you were only work?"

"Wasn't I?"

"No." Derrick shook his head vehemently. "Samona, I wouldn't have made love to you because of my job."

"What are you saying?"

Derrick blew out a frazzled breath. How hard could it be to tell a woman that he cared about her, truly and deeply? He closed the distance between them and decided to go for it. He had nothing to lose. Right now, he didn't have Samona and wouldn't unless he took a chance.

"I know this is going to sound strange, but hear me out. I'm not sorry about my undercover job." At her puzzled expression, he held up a hand. "If I hadn't had that assignment, I would never have met you. I would never have fallen for you."

Fallen for you . . . Samona wanted to cry. Instead, she

stared at him. If she was a fool for caring, then so be it. "Are you saying—"

"Yes." Derrick nodded. But he didn't actually say the words.

There was a sad expression in his eyes, and Samona's heart ached. But she couldn't go to him. Not until she had a few answers. "I know nothing about you. Not really."

"You know I'm not a writer. I'm a detective with the Chicago PD."

"But I know nothing else."

His gaze caressed her face. Somehow the energy between them had changed. It was no longer tentative. It was filled with sexual tension.

"Go ahead," Derrick said. "Ask me whatever you want to know. I'll tell you no lies."

"How long have you been a cop?"

Derrick reached out and cupped her chin. "Seven years."

It was hard to concentrate with him touching her. "I . . . I don't know how old you are."

"Twenty-nine. I'll be thirty in October."

"So I'm older than you."

"By eleven months and some days. You'll be thirty-one in November."

His gaze held her mesmerized. His touch made her body thrum. "That's not fair. You . . . you know everything about me."

Derrick shook his head. "No. I don't." He tangled his fingers in her hair. "Not everything."

"Like what?" she asked breathlessly. But she knew. She could see the question in his eyes.

"I don't know how you feel about me."

"I—" When his other hand touched her face, her breath snagged.

"I know you want me."

"I . . ." The pad of his thumb brushed her lip and for

a moment, Samona's eyes fluttered shut. She couldn't deny it. "I know I shouldn't, but I do."

"Do you forgive me?"

"I shouldn't. I should be mad at you forever."

He inched closer to her face. "But that wouldn't be any fun, now would it?"

"You don't play fair." Her arms must have had a mind of their own for they circled Derrick's waist.

Derrick moaned. "Neither do you." His lips brushed hers and Samona's parted in expectation. "Samona, I know we haven't known each other long. But what I feel for you . . . it's more than just sex. This is the real thing. You did something to me, Samona. Somehow, you took my heart. Believe me, that's not an easy thing to do."

She wanted him to stop this tortuous foreplay and kiss her. That was the last thing she should be thinking, but at this moment she knew she was crazy. Crazy for him. And despite what he had done she didn't want to live without him. How could she live without this?

Gently, he kissed her lips, then pressed his forehead against hers. He pulled her close and Samona could feel the evidence of his desire for her. She shuddered.

"I love you, Samona." He looked at her, his eyes honest, sincere. "And I'm hoping you love me too."

"I . . . yes." Her eyes misted. "Derrick, I do."

"Then kiss me. Hold me. Never let me go."

Molding her body to his, Samona did as he'd told her. She wrapped her arms tightly around him, ran her fingers up and down his back. Then slowly, she edged her lips close to his.

It was a sweet, slow kiss. A grateful kiss. A kiss filled with longing. A kiss that spoke of endings and new beginnings.

A kiss that promised many tomorrows.

EPILOGUE

It was the perfect day for a wedding.

It was warm, warmer than usual for the end of September, with just enough of a cool breeze to make the heat bearable. The sun smiled down at them from a cloudless sky, approving of this new union. Even the birds chirped and sang from the trees in Grant Park, as though happy for them.

Derrick nibbled on her ear. "What do you say we take off, go to our new house and christen every room. . . ."

"And leave before our reception?"

Derrick flashed her a charming smile. "Nobody will notice."

Samona chortled. "Oh yeah. They won't notice the woman in white dashing to the limo."

"All right. You have a point. But you just look so good that I can't wait to get you out of that dress." His hand went to her lower back.

"Not so fast." She put a hand on his chest to hold him

at bay. "This dress happened to cost a fortune, and I'm getting my money's worth."

"You already got that and more. Today you officially earned the title of most beautiful woman in the world."

"Oh, Derrick." Cupping his cheek, Samona planted a soft kiss on his lips. It was amazing how her life had changed. In just three months, she was a different person. The disastrous time in her life with Roger was now a distant memory. Roger had survived his gunshot wound but was in prison. He would be there for many years to come, along with his accomplices. Angelo Milano, knowing he faced the rest of his life in jail for the hit on his wife, had, while on bail, put a gun to his head and pulled the trigger. It was a tragic ending to a tragic story.

Samona stared at her new husband. Now, she had better days to look forward to. She had her job back at her old school. She and her sister were getting along well. She wouldn't have thought it a few months ago, but she had a new, wonderful life and was incredibly happy.

"Okay, everybody!" Evelyn yelled. She had taken charge today, and Samona was thankful for that. She couldn't have made all the arrangements on her own. "Before the bride and groom get carried away on the grass, I say we take a group picture!"

There were several chuckles among the guests, and blushing, Samona pulled away from Derrick. They, the wedding party and the guests hustled on the grass, grouping together near the spectacular flower garden. The photographer set up his camera.

Evelyn, her matron of honor, was to her immediate right. Then came Jennifer, a bridesmaid, beside whom was Derrick's longtime friend and also one of her bridesmaids, Whitney Jordan. To Derrick's left was Nick Burns, his best man. Next to Nick was her brother-in-law, Mark and Derrick's brother-in-law, Russell, both groomsmen. Everyone else crowded around them—Derrick's mother and sister;

Whitney's husband, Javar; Mrs. Jefferson and their many other friends who consisted of police officers and teachers.

Derrick placed a possessive hand around her waist and pulled her close just as the photographer said, "Everybody ready?"

"Yes," they all replied in unison, followed by laughter. The camera flashed.

"I think I blinked," Evelyn said. "Take another one."

The photographer did. He said, "Got it."

The crowd disbursed. Husbands found their wives. Girlfriends found their boyfriends. Children found their parents.

Samona watched it all in wonder.

Derrick cupped her chin and turned her face to him. He looked into her eyes. "In case you didn't know, you have made me the happiest man on earth."

"And you've made me the happiest woman. This is like a dream. . . ."

"It is a dream. One we made a reality."

Samona framed his face. He was right. This day was a dream come true.

Derrick drew her close and captured her lips in a lingering kiss. Around them, the guests applauded and whistled.

Breaking the kiss, Samona looked out at all the smiling faces. Smiling for her. For Derrick. Snuggling against her husband, she smiled back, happiness overwhelming her.

It was the perfect day, she thought. The perfect day for a celebration of love.

Kayla Perrin lives in Toronto, Canada with her husband of five years. She attended the University of Toronto and York University, where she obtained a Bachelor of Arts in English and Sociology and a Bachelor of Education, respectively. As well as being a certified teacher, Kayla works in the Toronto film industry as an actress, appearing in many television shows, commercials, and movies.

Kayla is most happy when writing. As well as novels, she has had romantic short stories published by the Sterling/MacFadden Group.

She would love to hear from her readers. E-mail her at: kaywriter1@aol.com. Mail letters to:

> Kayla Perrin
> c/o Toronto Romance Writers
> Box 69035
> 12 St. Clair Avenue East
> Toronto, ON Canada
> M4T 3A1

Please enclose a SASE if you would like a reply.

COMING IN MAY ...

SUMMER MAGIC   (1-58314-012-3, $4.99/$6.50)
by Rochelle Alers
Home economics teacher Caryn Edwards is renting a summer house on North Carolina's Marble Island. She was certain it would give her a chance to heal from her ugly divorce and career burnout. What she didn't bargain for was handsome developer Logan Prescott who would unexpectedly be sharing the house with her.

BE MINE   (1-58314-013-1, $4.99/$6.50)
by Geri Guillaume
Judie McVie has worked all her life on Bar M, her uncle's sprawling Mississippi ranch. When he died, they were sure he'd left them the land. But mysterious loner Tucker Conklin appeared with the will in hand, claiming the ranch. She'd do anything to hold onto her family's legacy ... and he'd do anything to capture her heart.

MADE FOR EACH OTHER   (1-58314-014-X, $4.99/$6.50)
by Niqui Stanhope
Interior designer Summer Stevens is hoping to escape Chicago and throw herself into work at a Jamaican beach cottage owned by the wealthy Champagne family. But focusing on business proves to be a challenge when she meets her devilishly attractive employer, Gavin Pagne.

AND OUR MOTHER'S DAY COLLECTION ...

A MOTHER'S LOVE   (1-58314-015-8, $4.99/$6.50)
by Candice Poarch, Raynetta Mañees and Viveca Carlysle
No woman is as loved or as loving as a mother, and our authors help honor that special woman. "More Than Friends," by Poarch, "All the Way Home," by Mañees, and "Brianna's Garden," by Carlysle, three short stories of extraordinary mothers in search of love.

ble wherever paperbacks are sold, or order direct from the isher. Send cover price plus 50¢ per copy for mailing and handing to BET Books, c/o Kensington Publishing Corp., Consumer Orders, or call (toll free) 888-345-BOOK, to place your order using Mastercard or Visa. Residents of New York, Washington D.C. and Tennessee must include sales tax. DO NOT SEND CASH.

SPICE UP YOUR LIFE
WITH ARABESQUE ROMANCES

AFTER HOURS, by Anna Larence   (0-7860-0277-8, $4.99/$6.50)
Vice president of a Fort Worth company, Nachelle Oliver was used to things her own way. Until she got a new boss. Steven DuCloux was ruthless—and the most exciting man she had ever known. He knew that she was the perfect VP, and that she would be the perfect wife. She tried to keep things strictly professional, but the passion between them was too strong.

CHOICES, by Maria Corley   (0-7860-0245-X, $4.95/$6.50)
Chaney just ended with Taurique when she met Lawrence. The rising young singer swept her off her feet. After nine years of marriage, with Lawrence away for months on end, Chaney feels lonely and vulnerable. Purely by chance, she meets Taurique again, and has to decide if she wants to risk it all for love.

DECEPTION, by Donna Hill   (0-7860-0287-5, $4.99/$6.50)
An unhappy marriage taught owner of a successful New York advertising agency, Terri Powers, never to trust in love again. Then she meets businessman Clinton Steele. She can't fight the attraction between them—or the sensual hunger that fires her deepest passions.

DEVOTED, by Francine Craft   (0-7860-0094-5, $4.99/$6.50)
When Valerie Thomas and Delano Carter were young lovers each knew it wouldn't last. Val, now a photojournalist, meets Del at a high-society wedding. Del takes her to Alaska for the assignment of her career. In the icy wilderness he warms her with a passion too long denied. This time not even Del's desperate secret will keep them from reclaiming their lost love.

FOR THE LOVE OF YOU, by Felicia Mason   (0-7860-0071-6, $4.99/$6.50
Seven years ago, Kendra Edwards found herself pregnant and alone. Now she has a secure life for her twins and a chance to finish her college education. A long unhappy marriage had taught attorney Malcolm Hightower the danger of passion. But Kendra taught him the sensual magic of love. Now they must each give true love a chance.

ALL THE RIGHT REASONS, by Janice Sims   (0-7860-0405-3, $4.99/$6
Public defender, Georgie Shaw, returns to New Orleans and meets reporte
Knight. He's determined to uncover secrets between Georgie and her c
twin, and protect Georgie from someone who wants both sisters dead.
ous secrets are found in a secluded mansion, leaving Georgie with no on
trust but the man who stirs her desires.

*Available wherever paperbacks are sold, or order direct from the
Publisher. Send cover price plus 50¢ per copy for mailing and
handling to Kensington Publishing Corp., Consumer Orders,
or call (toll free) 888-345-BOOK, to place your order using
Mastercard or Visa. Residents of New York and Tennessee
must include sales tax. DO NOT SEND CASH.*

WARMHEARTED AFRICAN-AMERICAN ROMANCES
BY *FRANCIS RAY*

FOREVER YOURS   (0-7860-0483-5, $4.99/$6.50)
Victoria Chandler must find a husband or her grandparents will call in loans
that support her chain of lingerie boutiques. She fixes a mock marriage to
ranch owner Kane Taggert. The marriage will only last one year, and her
business will be secure. The only problem is that Kane has other plans for
Victoria. He'll cast a spell that will make her his forever.

HEART OF THE FALCON   (0-7860-0483-5, $4.99/$6.50)
A passionate night with millionaire Daniel Falcon, leaves Madelyn Taggert
enamored . . . and heartbroken. She never accepted that the long-time family
friend would fulfill her dreams, only to see him walk away without regrets.
After his parent's bitter marriage, the last thing Daniel expected was to be
consumed by the need to have her for a lifetime.

INCOGNITO   (0-7860-0364-2, $4.99/$6.50)
Owner of an advertising firm, Erin Cortland witnessed an awful crime and
lived to tell about it. Frightened, she runs into the arms of Jake Hunter, the
man sent to protect her. He doesn't want the job. He left the police force after
a similar assignment ended in tragedy. But when he learns not only one man
is after her and that he is falling in love, he will risk anything to protect her.

ONLY HERS   (07860-0255-7, $4.99/$6.50)
St. Louis R.N. Shannon Johnson recently inherited a parcel of Texas land.
She sought it as refuge until landowner Matt Taggart challenged her to prove
she's got what it takes to work a sprawling ranch. She, on the other hand,
soon challenges him to dare to love again.

SILKEN BETRAYAL   (0-7860-0426-6, $4.99/$6.50)
The only man executive secretary Lauren Bennett needed was her five-year-old
son Joshua. Her only intent was to keep Joshua away from powerful in-laws.
Then Jordan Hamilton entered her life. He sought her because of a personal
vendetta against her father-in-law. When Jordan develops strong feelings for
Lauren and Joshua, he must choose revenge or love.

ENIABLE   (07860-0125-9, $4.99/$6.50)
Texas heiress Rachel Malone defied her powerful father and eloped
Logan Williams. But a trump-up assault charge set the whole town and
Rachel against him and he fled Stanton with a heart full of pain. Eight years
later, he's back and he wants revenge . . . and Rachel.

*Available wherever paperbacks are sold, or order direct from the
Publisher. Send cover price plus 50¢ per copy for mailing and
handling to Kensington Publishing Corp., Consumer Orders,
or call (toll free) 888-345-BOOK, to place your order using
Mastercard or Visa. Residents of New York and Tennessee
must include sales tax. DO NOT SEND CASH.*

LOOK FOR THESE ARABESQUE ROMANCES